SLIME TIME

A novella by Mackenzie Rice

To Grandma Pat, the woman who did so much to keep me inspired and fed.

To my parents, who fought for food and helped me live.

To my sister, whose judgment was always kind.

To my wife, who I love more than life itself.

And, to everyone who reads; Sorry!

Mackenzie is a disabled transgender woman living in Vancouver, Canada, on unceded Coast Salish (xʷməθkʷəy̓əm (Musqueam), Sḵwx̱wú7mesh (Squamish), and Səlilwətaɬ (Tsleil-Waututh)) Land.

Contents

CONTENT WARNINGS

VIOLENCE
- Blood, Bodily harm, Mild gore, Extreme gore, Crush implication, Murder (non-permanent, consensual), Police violence implication

MEDICAL
- Scalpels, Surgery, Exploration, Nausea, Regurgitation, Medical system mismanagement, Genital trauma

KINK
- Micro, Macro, Vore, Digestion implication, Esoteria (cybernetic enhancements, mentions of abstract kinks, etc), Generally lots of sex, honestly

ABUSE
- Child abuse, Personal manipulation, Mental trauma

ETC.
- Death (temporary), Reclaimed slurs, Intense descriptions of disassociation, Descriptions of reactions to trauma, Queer trauma, Drug usage

MAJOR THEMES ARE -
- Queer Trauma
- Communist Aesthetic Appropriation
- Sex and Identity
- Systemic Abuse
- General Dystopia

Lost

4:30 a.m.

The sky was overcast with the bubbly black of a storm meant for somewhere else down the jetstream, with CRT scanline colors of projected advertisements angled for viewers a half hour away by train coloring the downward swells above the quay. A small starry broke through the cover above the bay, its gleaming underside reflecting for a moment all those colors and products around it like a mirror ball. The vapor trail from the sky clung to it as the reentry heat patina crept along its underside, tag-team muting the display and costing someone somewhere a few million dollars in lost advertising.

Kyle was alone.

A breeze whipped at her clothes, at her fur, and she didn't know if it was the starry's dramatic maneuvering above the water in the distance or the storm's breath rolling by. Kyle took the cigarette out of her mouth and flicked it over the guardrail on the bridge, somewhere in the general direction of the quay, the starry, the "people" no-doubt shouting on phones and threatening to sue for a maybe-sum of maybe-money that might-have-been-lost. Debt accrued, not to be recouped. Fuck them. How dare they intrude on a girl's contemplation time next to the endless sea.

The sight of the fading arc of red in the night provided little comfort.

Kyle's phone buzzed against her thigh, and for a second she thought she'd be sick. She choked back the nugget of bile that taunted her esophagus and slid her hand in to grab it, feeling a few smoldering cig flakes scrape off and get stuck in the fabric.

Red thoughts, black spite, a spike of heated hate through her chest. Matching emotions to the tiny whisper of "God *fucking* dammit" out of her short muzzle. Against the physical medium of her skin and the denim shorts, they sputtered out faster than she could even grab her phone, but the echo of pain lingered. She accepted the call without looking to see the number.

"Who's calling?"

"Hey, this is Josiah from Bunton Heights Public Health, you're Kyle O., right?"

"Yeah, speaking. Uh." She winced.

"You're Bennett's contact, right?"

"Uh." *Who the fuck is Bennett?* "Yeah, what's up?"

"He's alright, he just asked for assistance getting home. A little delirious, you know."

"Right. What's the address again?"

"Five-two-nine-four South Quail Terrace, Bunton Heights, BC. You sure you don't need to come in for yourself?"

The receptionist's voice was unusually chipper and attempting fun for this time of night. They must've been having a fucking boring shift.

"I'm good. Tell Benny I'll be there in..."

She looked around, predator's eyes well-attuned to the darkness; urban light pollution helped. She looked down and around among the jungle of skyscrapers and more squat buildings, tracing her path to where she knew Bunton Heights was - funnily enough, in a commercial valley between house-encrusted hills. The Vancouver Special never went out of style, even as the population density spiked beyond belief. Some lucky fucks got to have half a house to themselves.

"...an hour, give or take."

Give or take how much my fucking mind wanders.

"Gotcha, Miss O. See you then."

"Bye."

Ugh.

Kyle put her phone back, a smooth motion in a tight pocket, save for the remaining carbonized grit from her cigarette. They weren't a concern, she was a few weeks from a new phone, and her denim shorts were already ripped. More concerning was the state of her bike and helmet.

Besides the breeze and ever-present nothing-everything-noise of the city down the hill, the only thing Kyle heard was the soft crunch of asphalt-gravel under her sneakers as she walked over to her bike. It was a skinny thing, intentionally resembling some classic off-roader from the old 90s, but weighed down with an excessive engine, clearly reaching past the original undercarriage. The flat plastic and metal bits were adorned with vintage counterculture stickers and shit, all black and red and white.

The left side's paint job and patches were half sheared off, though, to match the vicious run up Kyle's stockings and blood-matted fur beneath. She did her best to ignore the pain as she swung up and over, her left leg neatly covering the one patch of unmutilated expression. Kyle grit her teeth, dug her heel in, and got the hog roaring again. She gripped the handlebars, leaned forward, and let the bike lurch forward into a cruise. Let it take her away from her lonesome, down the road toward the lights on the other side of the hill.

It wasn't long before she was regretting cutting her self-reflection short. That hill was the one undeveloped bit of gravel and trees, an oasis of insulated calm and darkness, save for the creeping peeking ever-glow of the surrounding urban nightmare. One of the few places to look out and see the sky, unlatched from the businessmen's spires clawing at the belly of the night.

Some nights you could even see the stars. Not this morning, though. Only clouds that helped create the hazy midnight light that surrounded her again as she revved well above the speed suggestions, down the road and into the sleepy surrounding neighborhoods.

The streets were remarkably silent, even for that time of night, and especially so down near Bunton (not-so-)Heights and its generally thriving sex and hyperkink scenes. Normally there'd be at least a few businessmen with bedraggled clothes, drops of blood running from a popped stitch or bile or cum as souvenirs from their one-night fling.

Kyle hit a red light and slow-rolled through it, wary but aware. A bus, parked by its lonesome beneath a sickly orange lamp, was the only other motor running in ear or eyeshot. Only one person's footsteps were clunking loudly as she crossed the intersection, belonging to a gasping businessperson with broad shoulders and an unbuttoned fly, practically dripping with the skunk scent of femmy jizz. She hit the brakes and grinned ear to ear.

"Heyyyy, Nine-To-Five! Better get some sleep or the boss'll know you were sex fuckin' instead of burnin' the midnight oil!" she called.

"Thanks, prick! Bet you wouldn't know about that! I hope you can afford your next oil change!" they called back, hoarse, spit dripping down their bottom lip.

"Nah," she called back, leaning forward to make sure she had the last word, "I get the five-finger discount! Good luck!"

The echo of screeching tires carried for miles, but she only heard them fresh in her ears. Her tires. Her noise. Her peel-out smear of melted rubber that would piss off the small store owners and their nepotic employees in their hundred-square-foot fiefdom. Anything less than pristine asphalt was bad for business.

She imagined them getting together, doing some honest fucking labor for the first time in months, to scrape away the streak on the street. A slideshow of petty lords coming together for their mutual benefit, and not fucking *getting* how easy it is to do shit without a paycheck.

Whatever. Maybe they'll get their places burned down.

Hope so.

Lost in thought, Kyle didn't notice the clinic's faux-neon sign hanging overhead until she stopped at a crosswalk and saw its sickly red reflection on the slick street below. With gritted teeth and an angrily hissed *"Shit,"* she leaned her weight on her mauled left leg, turned the handles, and gently, illegally, puttered across the lanes to enter the empty parking lot. Empty save for one *ancient*-looking JDM, tucked away in the unlit corner where the back of the clinic and the tower behind it met. She could smell leaking oil, and parked what she thought were two spots away - the formerly yellow paint had long cracked and faded away.

Her bike leaned heavily on the stand, the freshest-looking thing in the neighborhood besides the new blood gleaming against her leg.

Must've broken open a clot.

Kyle was more concerned about washing out her shoe when she got home. She consciously ignored the sensation of her leg splitting in half every time she took a step, tried not to focus on the tacky feeling of half-dried blood sticking her shoe to the ground, tried not to squint when the overhead sign's searing medicine-red light slammed into her eyes as she rounded the corner toward the entrance.

She lifted a hand dumbly halfway up her chest, just to let it drop. A proactive action that meant nothing, pre-fired neurons fizzling when she saw nothing she expected. The sidewalk was dirty, grimy, sure, but it looked power-washed - only the barest ghosts of stains lingered, imprinted in the worn-down concrete. Her dripping additions were the only things that looked even months recent. Little drops fell from the weighed-down laces of her shoes to soak into porous years of civil history.

The windows weren't broken like she remembered, either. They didn't exactly look fresh, little patinas of dust clinging to the mounded glue in the corners. The red reflected wasn't as vibrant, wasn't as-

Why the fuck am I psychoanalyzing this place?

She turned abruptly and leaned into her walk to the front. She couldn't be in the right place. This was a clinic, sure, but she was going to need directions to the *right* clinic. The door slid open to the left, and she turned in to the right to the most shocking sight yet.

Clean floors and walls, everything above ankle-level practically gleaming. The monitors hanging above the front table weren't burned in, but there was a film of dust along the top. Everything was too new. She looked down, saw a little grout in a tiny crack in the floor that nobody would ever notice again. Not new enough.

It even *smelled* clean. Not like the familiar smell of bleach not-quite masking blood and shit, just like a few hours after a mop. *Normal.*

No patients sitting around and bleeding out and whimpering near-death was the most damning observation. There wasn't even a fucking staffer there to triage kinksters through, either with glazed-over eyes or ones brimming with restrained tears. This couldn't have been the place that saw the churning masses coming through for recombination after visiting the Circus. No way Hell was here.

Besides the obvious waiting room atmosphere, it felt more like an abandoned school at night. Felt bad. Wrong place, wrong time. Kyle edged back towards the entrance, stepping back into a puddle of her own gory ichor with a gentle splash just loud enough to mask the hiss of a staff-only door sliding to let a worker through.

They called from the back of the desk with the chipper tone of someone who actually *likes* the night shift, for some ungodly reason.

"Welcome to the Bunton Heights Clinic, how may we help you today, Comrade?"

Ugh, here we go.

Kyle shot a wince-smile-wave to the clean-looking guy behind the counter - guy because she saw the pronouns on the nametag, just below Josiah Gertennbeg and the hammer-and-sickle lapel pin - and pretended to not have a limp when she stepped closer. At least she pretended not to notice it.

"You got, ah, a Bennett here?"

"Absolutely! He's waiting in recovery room A, down the hall and to the left. Watch your step, though!"

"Yeah, sure, thanks kadet. Iz nom bog, or whatever."

Kyle watched him furrow his brows in confusion, then look her up and down - then freeze when he looked below her belt.

"Uhm... excuse me, but, have you noticed your leg?"

"I'm trying not to think about it," she muttered truthfully.

"Can I... fix that up for you?"

"I guess that's your job. Grab your kit or whatever and I'll meet you in A."

Kyle turned from the desk and walked face-first into a motorless door, rubbed her nose, then manually pushed it to the side to step through into the patient-only rooms beyond - which were, really, just more of the exact same. More used-clean walls and chairs with only the faintest cracks in the leather, more spotted-spotless smooth-tile floors that clicked under the faded rubber of her right shoe and squelch-stuck under the drying mat of her own blood on her left. More of the Canadian leaf-and-hammer-and-sickle flags dangling from strings hung from the spackled ceiling, half of whom wiggled rapidly under the HEPA vents, the other half which did so slowly in synchronous polyrhythm.

The secretary-doctor-whatever hurriedly caught up with her, nothing in his hands except two limp teal latex gloves.

"You're, uh, leaking on the floor," he muttered, looking over his shoulder while she trudged on.

"No shit," she hissed, far more angrily than she thought she would.

The spikes of pain were piercing higher on every step. When she walked in, they were only reaching up to her hip. Now they were starting to poke at her clenched neck.

"Some of your flesh is hanging off. I'm going to, uh, have to cut away some of your jeans."

Fuck, she thought with enough hatred to get the same "Fuck" out of her own mouth.

"I just ripped these up last week," she continued.

"Well," he started, in a consoling-helping tone, "you can wash them and put them back together even more punk...ily?"

"Yeah."

"Yeah! I love your retro look. Real 2020s black denim revival stuff!"

Kyle sniffed, crinkled her snout. That was enough of *that* conversation.

Around one more bend were the recovery rooms, A, B, C, arranged in a neat little triplet against the back wall. For some reason, the designer had neglected one additional light in the ceiling, which cast the three little cards above the doors in an inexplicably unnecessary shadow. The medical red and white dimmed to a deep crimson and an off-pink in the dark. Kyle did what she did best - actively ignore the ominous details - and strode up to room A's door, same as all the others.

"Alright, we got a Bennett in here?" she called, pulling the door open to look inside.

A small voice returned, halfway between the sound of a striking match and the squeak of a gerbil, with the tone of a recovering drunk.

"Oh my *god*, Kyle T. Orlanski, you actually came!"

A wave of sudden recognition hit her. The memory of his nebulous form rolled over her brain like one of those classic screeching slow-brake chugga-chugga trains, and the hot wave of shame followed, from scalp down. The room's appearance didn't even register in her brain until Josiah gripped her shoulder and pulled her out of her momentary trance.

"Uh, Ms. Orlanski, you're- are you going to pass out?"

She blinked, then shot a hateful look at the secre-whatever beside her again.

"Blood loss," she hissed, then entered the recovery room with him in tow.

It was simple. A medical-grade futon on one side, a bed on the other, a chair in the middle, with a bathroom and a sink in the back. There were a few dribbles of fluid on the ground next to the chair, a grimy ocher that glimmered in the dim light only for a second, when it caught her bleary eye. In the chair was a man no taller than four inches tall, that she unfortunately remembered extremely well.

"Yeah, uh, I don't remember you," she lied. "Bennett, was it?"

She kept her eyes closed to picture him instead of looking. Picture where she met him.

Drunk to fuck, bass crunching and blowing out cheap speakers. Venue for fifty, packed to three hundred. Everyone's conversations loud as screams, overlapping. Red. Black. The band sucked, so they put on someone's playlist over the wifi. Alcohol clung to her throat and her hair covered her eyes as she verbally taunted another furry not even as big as her four-dollar rip-off hot dog. Thin-looking guy, handsome stripes and retracted claws, looking about as scared as if she just said she was going to-

Kyle opened her eyes, hoping and praying that it was some different loser.

Grinning at her from the middle of the room, roles reversed, was Bennett the tiger. Thin shoulders, long hair, fishnet leggings and a tight crop-top. Just like that night. Just the same as if she'd never-

"Kyle, Kyle! Come on now!" he called across several feet of space, clearly straining his throat to be heard over the beating heat in her ears that he *somehow* knew was there. His voice had a lilt in it that suggested the sleepy-time surgery drugs or whatever the fuck were still pumping around in his sluggish blood.

"Mr. Quail, uh, knew your contact information. I think you two know each other."

Kyle turned to death-stare the secretary into dust, but the little shit in the spotlight didn't skip a beat, even with the opiates.

"Of course we do! We met-"

"Bennett-" she hissed, whipping back around. Her bad leg shook.

"-at a cool party! She was drunk as *hell*, though, that's why she doesn't remember it."

Kyle wished she could breathe a sigh of relief. A half second of calm to let her guard down before he twisted the fucking knife in, making it *so* much worse.

"She wanted to eat me, so - I obliged!"

Her heart stopped in her chest. Bennett's voice seemed ever more tiny, ever more distant as her brain distanced her from the world. A subconscious pat-pat there-there freezing disconnect as that little shit kept going in his squeaky little fucking voice.

"She's got a pretty intense vore kink, which, you know, that's *cool*, but I was expecting to do something way, way harder than that!"

Josiah gingerly shouldered past Kyle, the gentle brush nearly knocking her off her feet.

"Well, Ms. Orlanski, I guess I misjudged you a little!"

Her hair hung over one of her eyes, but both of them were wide in shock.

*They think I'm a fucking **loser**.*

"I was kind of a mess the next day, but - well! Here I am!"

The tiger-man chuckled and put his hands behind his head. He wiggled triumphantly, if dozily, like he'd just finished a mildly difficult puzzle or humiliated the one person he could think of to call to help him.

"That was months ago," Kyle said hoarsely, raising one hand to point limply at him. A non-gesture. A grasping-for-something gesture.

"Oh! Yeah, I, hahaha, I'm here because I had to get recombinated after - well, I don't know if your tummy can handle hearing it, Kyle."

He turned his little head to Josiah, who was smirking a little, comfortable, finally, around these two fuzzy weirdos who just weren't *that* weird.

"Try me," she croaked, leaning forward. On her bad leg.

Making a fucking point.

Bennett's smile faded. Maybe. It was hard to tell, halfway across the room, when he was only a few inches tall.

"That's what I thought," she said, not moving her jaw to do so. Anger kept her teeth clenched.

"…no offense, Kyle," Josiah started, suddenly feeling cozy enough to start calling a patient by her first name, "but with your attitude I thought you'd be into something more extreme. Public flogging, amputation, railway suicide-sex-"

Kyle *slammed* her hand into the doorframe, head hanging forward in her best approximation of what she thought would scare the everloving shit out of this mild-mannered med school half-grad.

He blinked, but didn't flinch.

"I'm sorry ma'am, but you're going to have to back up the threat *sometime*."

Josiah motioned to the futon, folded up against the wall, and then to the ominously worn red brick of a device hanging on the wall at its foot. She darted her tongue out to wet her lips, her mouth suddenly very dry.

"Fine," Kyle croaked. She moved away from the wall with a very prominent limp, but her not-quite-steps left behind far less blood than the ones down the hallway. She turned and slumped against the futon, its beige surface crinkling expectedly, if uncomfortably.

Josiah put his professional airs on, sauntering past the two to the wall to pluck that ominous kit from its hook on the wall.

Heavy plastic and metal clunked together. Muffled. A hint of glass. Instrumentation made to be thrown around like a suitcase. The hairs on Kyle's neck rose, but she didn't move. She didn't know if staring down the barrel or squirming nervously would be the bigger tell.

"Now," Josiah said, triumphantly, holding the densely packed device at his side, "if you'd be so kind as to extend your leg."

Her eyes locked with his. It took a moment, but Kyle willed limp muscles that had fully given up their swagger to shift once more. She flicked her eyes down to make sure her numb leg was actually fully extended. There was a greasy trail of blood and something else where her shoe had slid along.

She heard the snap of latex gloves coming on, and the clunk of that nameless-to-her device rested on the floor.

Josiah reached into a pocket and pulled out ever-classic medical scissors, sharper than a razor and meaner-looking than her own designer fangs.

The answer is not to move. Don't fucking move.

The doctor lifted the bottom of her shorts, caked at the hem with blood, and cut directly up the leg. Clinical, simple, easy. Practiced in a lab, not on people. She could tell by the inordinately ginger movements, not daring to brush a single finger anywhere near the sites of shorn skin and embedded gravel. Trophies from some asshole driver on the highway.

A stray pinky flicked across the vast scab, and a chunk of rubble fell off. The sound of its impact with the floor was hidden under the hiss of her pained teeth-suck.

"Do they let you keep shit like that anymore?" she joked, or tried, her voice stuck in her chest.

"No, sadly. I wish I had my tonsils," he returned dully.

"Tell you the truth, doc, I hate this part."

"You'll be okay."

They always say that.

Kyle shifted uncomfortably, unconsciously - *that* was the tell after all.

In the cramped room, with no-one speaking, it was very easy to hear the drip-drip leaky faucet of unhealthily deep red blood leaking out of the scabbed-over fur and onto the linoleum. Drip drip drip between the snip snip snip. A slab of crusty denim fell to the floor, landing in the puddle with a mix of a splash and a thunk.

He knelt down, careful to not touch the blood, and flicked open several latches, letting the device spring wide open. She kept her eyes on Josiah's eyes, though his attention was obviously elsewhere. She refused to acknowledge the corners of her vision catching the gleam of whatever self-sanitizing blades and hooks and tubes and whatever other horrible clinical devices lay arrayed in their open sheath.

Christ, I need a distraction.

"Hey, uh - you seem pretty fresh-faced, doc. Not a dig at your credentials. Isn't this the hyperkink block?"

Josiah reached for the wedge of medical nightmare, paused, shook his head, paused, then picked it up at both ends. Somewhere in the process he'd replaced his gloves. He placed the bottom at Kyle's ankle, and it closed automatically with a harsh plastic click and a foamy hiss.

"Jesus," Kyle hissed.

She looked up and away, trying to see why Bennett wasn't saying some more clown shit about all this. A tiny chest, rising and falling. No glimmer of open eyes. Restful, properly drugged sleep.

Jealous.

Another loud click, hiss, pressure around her thigh. Kyle couldn't bend her leg anymore, the plastic device bracing it tight. There really wasn't any room for medical panic anymore - she couldn't run if she wanted. Kyle felt a needle poke right into the sorest spot, crunching through dry blood and scab tissue, and gritted her teeth. The distinct warmth of fluid pulsing through ravaged flesh, inflamed tissue that begged for relief.

Everything was pretty cool after that, actually. Logically, she understood the random muted pressure as slicing, peeling, suction, stitching, cauterizing. The brick latched to her leg shook now and again, probably digging too deep, having to readjust on the fly. Modern marvel of medical technology pumping her full of drugs and sawing her apart.

It made a frighteningly loud *clunk* and Kyle's stomach turned over from the mix of gory thoughts and the painkillers hitting her gastro system. Her microbiosphere started throwing a wicked bender somewhere in her upper intestines, threatening to crash the party into the wish-it-was empty expanse of her stomach. She closed her eyes tight and flicked her head up to where she approximated she'd be otherwise looking at Josiah. Between heavy breaths to keep her dinner down, she asked him again -

"So, this *isn't* the hyperkink block?"

"No," the doctor muttered distantly, probably focused on her leg, "they had moved on before I got this assignment. Probably for the better, I'm a bit... nervous, squeamish."

Me too, pal.

"Did they get kicked out for disrupting the peace?"

"Probably. All I know is… I was given this post, told it was the stomping ground of Circus and Hell, and came out to a quiet street and a fresh coat of paint."

"Mmh. Lucky you, I guess. I'll have to…"

Kyle winced as one sharp stab of pain pushed deep through the wall of numbness. That lightning agony followed her nerves all the way up, and she folded her ears back as they started ringing.

"-f-find out where else to get my jollies."

"With how notable they are, I, ah, I'm sure you'll find them again."

"No doubt," she huffed.

The banging from the device stopped, and likewise did the riot in her gut peter out. For a moment she imagined a million million bruised and beaten hung-over microbes ashamedly marching home at the crack of dawn. Kyle opened her eyes to the doctor, his hands gently tugging on the ends of that horrible plastic lifesaver.

Hiss, click. It unlatched from her leg, and only a few stray tufts of freshly cleaned fur stuck to the device as he took it away to place back against the wall. She shivered at the last glimpse of gleaming medical metal before it snapped closed on itself, not to move again.

"Hate those things," she reiterated. Kyle reached her left hand down and ran the tips of her first two fingers through the fur, feeling the extraordinarily subtle bumps of subsurface stitches under the faintest line of sealed skin. Medical fucking marvel.

"Medical marvel that takes a lot away from the doctor-patient experience, if you ask me," Josiah added on cue.

Kyle acknowledged their synchronicity with a sharp nasal exhale.

"If you're done with me, then, I'll take Bennett and get going. Where's he live? Address on file, that shit?"

All the professional composure Josiah had leaned on fell out from under him the moment she asked. He lowered his head apologetically, mirroring the approximate anxiety that he'd displayed just a bit ago, before the swirling miseries compounded her down.

Kyle stood to her full height again, emotionally towering. Role reversal wasn't her biggest kink, but she could appreciate it in times like this.

"You don't know. Look it up," she rumbled.

"You're the only contact he knew. We didn't... don't, uh, have any files on hand, besides purely medical records."

She raised an eyebrow.

"You're kidding."

"N...no. No address on file, no family."

"So you called me at -"

Kyle pulled out her phone to look at the time, then put it back. Still gritty in the pocket. She pretended not to have forgotten to take it out before he'd started cutting.

" - four-thirty or so, in the morning, to be a valet for one of your patients."

Shouldn't he have called the pigs about this one?

A pause. The visual idea of a jackboot crushing a man over and over and over and-

Kyle's cock pulsed once in her shorts. She sneered to herself, her stomach flipping once at the thought of even beginning to enjoy that, and a second time as some sleepless microbe in her second brain banged on the roof to keep it the fuck down out there.

No. Actually I'm glad he didn't.

Doc's hands were pressed together, finger between finger, tight enough the skin was pale white and the knuckles were bright red.

"Fine. I'll, uh, drive around a while until he recovers enough to wake up again, alright?"

Josiah visibly wilted, a broken smile crossing his tender, pink face. He didn't seem like a bad guy. Just a med student way out of his league and way too high on that medical professional megalomania. Kyle's glare softened on its own, but she refused to smile. She turned to the middle chair one more time, extended a hand, and plucked Bennett up.

So small. So delicate. He felt like a purring doll in her hand, bones of toothpicks and an articulated spine more fluid than solid between her thick fingers. He was fucking snoring.

Kyle nonchalantly tucked him into her jacket's left pocket, right above her heart. For the first time in a long time, she clicked the button to keep something in place up there.

"Thank you," Josiah muttered.

"If you can help it, I wasn't here tonight," she returned, turning to walk out the door.

"Why?"

"Same reason you didn't call someone more *qualified*."

She turned back to watch his imagination mull over the thought of a man crushed under a jackboot again and again and again and then look back up at her with his bottom lip shaking.

"I'll figure something out, Ms- Whoever You Are."

Kyle nodded, gave him a thumbs-up, and walked away. She followed the trail of her own dried blood back out front, adding a few faded prints with the still-sticky sole of her left shoe.

The night was a little less dark outside. An inexplicable gray filter over everything that still made the details of the parking lot a little more defined. The beginning of morning, the sun's barest rays reflected off a thousand polished and patinated surfaces to reach her eyes in the foggiest way.

It was just a little too warm. She'd been up all night, and the normal her body had adapted to in that time was much chillier than even the tip of the day's temperature ahead. The weight of the night's exhaustion pressed down on her shoulders. She rolled them forward defiantly.

Kyle traced her steps back to her bike and turned and leaned against it. Without the subtle pain of her leg, all of its loving textures came back to her in new detail. The harsh grit of the scraped-up side against her bare legs. The subtle heat-warping of the chromed pipes against her calves. She lifted a hand to the handlebar - hard, barely yielding rubber, indented from hundreds of hours of her grip - inhaled, and sighed.

This was the one fucking thing in this world Kyle could rely on.

Bennett stirred in her pocket, and she snapped out of her object-worship. Only utility, now. With practiced abandon, Kyle turned around and lifted her leg over the side, kicked up the stand, dug in her heels, and felt sweet rolling power propel her out of the parking lot and into the last vestiges of the lingering night.

Something else stirred in the primal emotive gut between her heart and her stomach. Intangible fear. Terror-as-worry, bad vibes on a deeply instinctual level.

She didn't hit a red light for miles.

2

Found

6:01 a.m.

The sun was fully beginning its streak across the clear summer sky, that roaring ball of essential fire diffused into a vague yellow-red smear through the layers of the atmosphere both natural and artificial. If one stood in a field and looked to the very corners of the sky, you might see some gleaming shafts of perfect light, reflected without dilution - but Kyle lived in the city, boxed-in by the mountains to two sides. It had been a very, very long time since she had seen even a glimpse of the pure sun in the sky.

Vancouver was slowly coming to life around Kyle. People of all stripes stepped out of their abodes, checking wallets, phones, badges, pants and overall buttons, and some even came together at the bus station at the corner opposite her parking spot in an empty lot. She watched with a mesmerized exhaustion this pre-crowd of people who existed just to get things ready for the people just waking up. Bleary-eyed essentials milling on the streets under the gazes of even more people leaning out their windows, filling the air with the mingled reek of their tobacco and weed.

Kyle inhaled the last ashy bits of her own cigarette and took the nub from her lips, then exhaled and added her contribution to the chorus of smells to send off those first-shift geeks who would never get more genuine affection than this.

The bus pulled up, a little more lethargic than usual. The silhouette of the driver sat bolt upright, not leaning in their seat; a first-first shifter, taking it easy for a bit, letting the bus warm up before having to hit the real deadlines and schedules those freaks ashing their fags on windowsills and stepping back inside for their own mornings demanded.

Everyone stepped on the bus, and it rolled away, the driver's caution superseding anyone's need to get anywhere at any speed. Kyle was left thinking just how many millions of gallons of piss got flushed away between the hours of 5 and 8 in the morning.

What a waste.

Something else stirred with the urine cycle of the on-average 50 million first-shifters. Kyle tilted her snout down and gave a sidelong glance to the squirming man in her vest pocket.

"Good morning, sunshine," she croaked.

"I feel like I've slept a year," Bennett returned. Two tiny arms pushed out and hefted his tiny body up to lean over the bottom hem of the pocket like a railing.

"It's been about two hours, actually."

"No wonder I'm still tired."

Another bus rolled up across the street to pick up a few stragglers, not actually fully coming to a stop to open the doors before sailing away with a new impetus. The morning was actually starting.

"Where are we?"

Kyle placed a hand on her other vest pocket, finger tracing the crumpled bottom of her rapidly depleting pack of cigs. Tempting herself with another before breakfast. Denying herself was the strongest thing she could do.

"We're somewhere on Petro street. Truth be told, I've just been driving around with you in my pocket since the clinic."

She could barely tell the change in his expression through the corner of the one eye that was actually able to see him.

"Where the fuck's Petro street?"

"This used to be a suburb. They changed the name when they came through and turned it all to row houses and small businesses. I think the road used to be called Hoskins or some shit."

"Oh."

Bennett shifted in her pocket. Legs and torso moving behind a wall of stiff denim.

"Where are we going?"

You fucking tell me, dipshit.

Kyle forced herself to be a bit more diplomatic.

"Where do you live? I was gonna drop you off."

"Oh, that's..."

Kyle let him hold his pause for the length of three breaths.

"Well?"

His tone was more of a size-appropriate squeak than his normal boldness.

"That's a really good question, Kyler."

Kyle frowned, sneered, knitted her brow. An encompassing facial revulsion.

"Kyle."

"Kyle! Right, uh, Kyle. I'm sorry, I think - I think I might need some more sleep."

"Okay."

"Nothing... nothing's coming to me, uhm."

She set her molars, trying not to fully clench her teeth or to raise her voice or to grab him from her pocket and whip him into the street or stick him to one of her bike's brake pads and turn him into red paint at the first stoplight - but all those horrible thoughts helped calm her spiked heartbeat, at least.

"I'll figure it out for you. I know a guy. After that we'll get breakfast."

Bennett noticeably drooped in her pocket.

"I'm *so* fucking hungry..." he murmured, words that formed in her head after he said them, so quiet as to be a whisper underneath the gentlest city breeze.

"I have to wait 'till at least seven or eight to get breakfast."

"Why?"

"You'll see. Go back to sleep."

"Okay."

The tiger-man turned his head to look up at her for the first time. No sarcasm, no cheeky wit. Just a faded half-smile of someone ashamed and anxious and exhausted, approximated across a thick designer snout. She let her own expression soften.

"Go back to sleep."

Bennett nodded, hesitated, looked across the street at nothing and nobody. He let his arms slip a little, and he fell back into her pocket with the world's tiniest *flump*.

Kyle worked her jaw side to side, craving another death-stick's nicotine to ward away her creeping dread. Her mind and body began to work asynchronously, hands reaching out for handlebars and one leg swinging over the seat of her bike, while inside she scratched off a few options from her list of things to do that day. Her leg swung back and the kickstand flipped up, while she mentally circled and stabbed the next thing in line.

Talk to Aleks, doxx Bennett.

Unless she wanted to go pay fuck-you money to some larping 'detective' with a tan coat and a (somehow) legally acquired .460 who would dump both their personal info to the feds, she had to go to someone who could do things just as dubiously and a lot more discretely. While Kyle had never actually needed the guy in mind for more than some basic identity spoofing, she knew he had some *real* software and hardware under the trunk.

More importantly, however, he owed her a favor. Neither of them actually remembered what it was, as far as she knew. Just some heartfelt thanks from a night of broken bottles and noses and dripping blood. A trip to the clinic and their stitching machines before someone got too far along and had to get recombinated.

One thing that was easy for her to remember, though, was his favorite morning drinking spot. A back alley on a street without a name, between a laundromat and an apartment building nobody ever seemed to enter or leave, in a spot with suspiciously good wi-fi. It was about a five minute drive, and every moment not focused on the slowly increasing morning traffic was spent thinking about how she was going to ask him for help without getting into a fight.

The best friends are the ones you can't stand.

Kyle took the correct turns on memory-instinct, including doubling back once on the sleepy road for good measure. For Aleks' peace of mind, rather than her own concern. The sound of years of used and abused pavement became tremendously evident in the moments leading up to her parking her bike just inside the alley, wheels crunching grit loudly down the topless tunnel to announce her presence to her 'friend.'

A man with pale skin and a handsome grin turned to meet Kyle's eyes, waving with two fingers while holding a can of something with a label too small to read that she knew through unfortunate experience was booze.

"Hey, Aleks," she called, walking toward him with hands in her pockets. He took a long slurp off his can instead of responding right away.

Probably bracing himself for me, too.

Kyle took the opportunity to look him over, refamiliarize herself with him, sat on his throne of worn-down wooden pallets, framed by laptops both closed and open, and an ice cooler that was filled with more water than ice *or* beer.

Still, he cut the most majestic figure of Western perfection - straight posture, broad shoulders, strong brow, short, light-black hair, a forward-jutting chin, pronounced cheekbones. There was not a single natural blemish on his face, no discoloration on his perfect complexion. You could expect to see a guy like this on posters advertising the New Nationalists or something.

So, as anyone with a soul would, he took the necessary steps to become unappealing, ramming metal bits all over every orifice he had and leaving black and red ink innocently proclaiming his hatred of himself and those that would embrace him boldly upon his skin.

He smiled wide enough when he dropped his can that she wondered how his face didn't split open and let his piercings jingle comically to the rainy earth.

"Heyyy, Kyle. Surprise seeing you out here this early."

His voice would've been at home in an infomercial back in the 20th century, selling some gizmo that a few hundred people could use and a few million could make fun of. Bennett squirmed in her chest pocket, drawing Aleks' attention with a small jingle of the metal button.

"Who's this?" Bennett squeaked. He waved one arm in a flaccid general gesture, as if Kyle would have no idea who he's talking about.

"Good morning, again. That's fucking Lugal-zage-si," she said, smirking.

He frowned and pointed two fingers at her, more playful than accusatory.

"Don't you make fun of me! I tried, I failed."

"Gotta get back at you for calling me wolf-girl all the time."

"Well - am I supposed to parse what artistic interpretation of *big dog* you are?"

Kyle closed her eyes, mouth open, suddenly tense. She spoke carefully, cooling off the words as they came.

"My body is modeled after a coyote, Aleks."

"Oh."

He stuck out his pierced bottom lip in appreciation, matching eyebrow raise. He continued;

"Well how'm I supposed to tell when you're all black fur like that?"

Ask, fuckhead.

Kyle squeezed her eyelids together strongly enough to create sparkles in her nerves and distort her vision for whole seconds once she let them open again.

"Don't worry about it. I'm just here for help."

"No shit, eh?" Aleks returned, leaning over to fish for another can in his personal melted ice pack. His voice mingled with the clacking of rounded-off cubes floating on top of a sea of their melted brethren.

"Need help hiding your pal there? Erasing some records, again?"

"Finding them, actually."

Aleks looked from Kyle's face, looming over him, to the pocket Bennett popped out of, and Kyle followed suit, expecting that little shit to have some opiate-drunk shithead comment. Nothing came. He was unmoving again, asleep.

Convenient.

The harsh crack of Aleks' can snapped the awkward silence. The sound of piercings-on-tin and a gentle slurp followed. He placed the can to his side, and pulled up one of the laptops, one with the fewest and newest stickers stuck to the back of its screen.

"Doxxing your pal there, huh? Your phone off? Did you take the long way around?"

Yes, no, yes.

Kyle tightened her lips.

"Yes, yes, yes. You know me, bud. I don't fuck around with the things that make you comfortable."

"Thanks for that. What's your friend's name and what do you need?"

"Bennett Quail, I don't think he has a middle name. Apparently he knew me from some party a while ago, found him at a clinic after getting recombinated. I need his address, mainly, but anything could help."

Whisper-quiet, professional typing on the integrated keyboard. Some skills never go out of need, and those never go out of practice.

"Shouldn't be too hard... I'll just set up the parameters and let it go. Shouldn't be longer than a few minutes."

Kyle whispered, short and sharp. She was impressed.

"What the hell kinda government intelligence agency shit you got there?"

She leaned in curiously, wanting to see a glimpse of the program's interface she knew she could never actually parse. Aleks turned the laptop away, his brows furrowing.

"Sorry, wolf-girl, just looking at it is illegal."

She snorted in response and leaned away. Her right hand came up of its own accord to fidget with the pack of cigs in her vest pocket.

"And what you're doing is double-illegal, right?"

He was fucking with the touchpad, not listening. He continued talking after a pause and a swift hit of what she could only assume was the enter key to set the ball rolling.

"It's an auto-trawler I scraped up from one of those yearly government declassifications they dump. I modified it a little to work with my own little botnet."

Aleks picked his beer back up and took a long draft. She spoke over the gentle jingle of draining fluid.

"Sounds pretty impressive. Do this a lot?"

He gulped down the last of the booze in his mouth, wiped his mouth on the back of his bare arm, and hunched forward.

"I try not to. I'm scared of the repercussions from our *glorious* revolutionary government."

Please don't get into it right now, dude.

There was a long pause while everyone tried their best not to speak. Aleks broke the icey silence with a quiet, bitter tone.

"Did you see how twisted it was in Russia?"

Kyle blinked.

"What? When? Was there something recent?"

Aleks shook his head, some piece of metal clicking against another. It sounded more like lacquer than chrome.

"After the fall of the USSR."

Kyle clenched her fists.

Here we go.

He continued; "You know? After the failure of the Red Terror, after the failure of the Man of Steel, after millions of deaths in allied defiance of fascism, that great nationalist hate mutated from centuries of masurbatory Rome-love - which won in the end.

"It won because as soon as that great," he lifted his hands and deeply air-quoted, "'Revolutionary' experiment collapsed, it fell right back into the groping hands of nationalism."

Kyle only noticed she was clenching her teeth when he paused to take a sip of his nearly depleted beer.

"And so we had to think. And we had to redefine the left, and in that time, the State, Capital, all that *shit* took deepest hold, and..."

He waved his hand vaguely toward the street. His beer jingled in the thin aluminum for her attention. Her eyes, tired, obedient, flicked up to a bit of color, flapping in the achy sunbeams of the morning. The Canadian maple leaf, symbol of the stolen land for hundreds of years, wreathed by the gold laurels of supposedly socialist grain.

"Aesthetics," he choked out, a word gasped through a film of alcohol in his taxed throat, "all bacterial reaction to the one great thing the world had to save itself. Absorb the enemy and make it yours. Mitochondria.

"All we have now are a few impoverished locales with *great* reading programs in the mountains of what used to be the Yew-Ess, and a few labor-fetishizing rump states huddled against our fucking borders."

She waited a long moment and slid her thumbs thoughtfully, anxiously, one over the other. The natural friction of her pads found no purchase in their feather-light strokes over her smooth, painted claws, as intended. Anxious worship of non-thought.

He hissed out once more; "Fucking *borders*."

"You done?" she asked, quietly.

"Oh. Sorry. Yeah." He didn't look at her.

"Yeah." She looked at her shoes.

"The little fucker's files should've come back by now."

His tone had totally changed, that broad smile returning with aplomb. It didn't bring 'wolf-girl' any comfort now, but she managed a small smile in return. Courtesy.

Aleks lifted his laptop into his lap and cleared his throat, but didn't speak. He pressed the dull touchpad, his expression inscrutable but rapidly changing. A kaleidoscope with fitting piercing clicks for each movement. Aleks' voice came out delicately;

"I regret to inform you, wolf-girl, that my search came up with nothing."

A slow blink. Her heart accelerated in place. An engine revving in neutral.

"Can you... run that by me again?"

Aleks turned his laptop screen toward her, and she leaned in. On an HTML file, among the 12,500-plus potential hits, 1100-plus strong hits, not a single corresponding line was drawn between any. It was a screen of neatly collated mass data that did not apply to the Bennett in her pocket at all.

"That's new."

Those were words Kyle Orlanski was not used to saying. They were words that made her slowly roll her long muzzle with exaggerated enunciation, as if some messenger of understanding or revelation would catch up to her sluggish words, pass them a note saying "Everything is okay!" and then she would be able to adjust course.

No-one came.

The pregnant pause following the end hung heavy like her open jaw.

"I should drink more," Aleks growled. A half-sigh half-hiss of gargled booze and barely restrained, riotous self-hatred. She could read it on his perfect, manually marred features; this was the only thing he had going on today - and he'd failed.

"I'm gonna drink more. I'm seeing double."

The few ice cubes left in the cooler jingled against his rings and the tin can of his booze he dredged up from the murk with expert precision.

"You sure you should be having another beer, Aleks?"

"Only way I can cope with the visions at this point," he returned. His shoulders slouched as he yet lifted the can - one among a dozen, the previous eleven-some littering the alleyway at his feet - to his mouth and gulped. He swayed. He didn't come up for air. His whole body sagged. He drained the can and it drained him, whatever little was left.

Kyle sighed out a sliver of her pent-up anxiety. She let her long fingers find their way fully into the pack of cigs on her chest, a desire animating beneath her swimming, conscious thoughts. They plucked one slightly bent stick between their index and middle members, then swerved down to pry out the lighter that made an indent in her torn up black shorts between their ring and pinky fingers.

Fine, fuck it.

She consciously cooperated with the forces of primal desire, half-animated movements practiced beyond thought. Filter to her lips, gentle grip, a strike of the lighter, a second's fragrance of burning butane immediately overtaken by tobacco and tar.

"Oh, fuck you bud, put that shit out around me."

Aleks whipped his can to the side, and it clattered hollowly along the graveyard of its fellows. He stood to his full height - probably six-foot-something - and menacingly strode toward her, the top of his head solidly level with her flat chest. She didn't stop smoking.

"Take your corporate death-shit outta this alley, kindly."

His voice was quiet, intense. Anger and a moment of false sobriety.

Quit lashing out on me, fuckhead.

"If you're allowed to get yourself shitted up before the commonfolks' breakfast time, then I'm allowed my corporate fucking death shit."

Kyle's voice was quiet, icy. A veneer she had to keep from snapping.

"God *dammit* Kyle," Aleks moaned, emotion welling up like vomit in the back of his throat. Her heart flipped in her chest. She refused the very human urge to help.

"You - you come in here and smoke, against my wishes, and you mock my contributions to the community, the, the *one community* trying for real autonomy, real, *real* mutual aid."

Calmly, but no less icily, Kyle responded through her clenched fangs;

"Take that up with the people, you fucking egomaniac."

"No!"

Kyle squinted, feeling her heavy brows strain with the mixed emotions of confusion and anger. She just let him continue.

"All of them! All of them failed, Kyle! I was the last *fucking* one putting my ass on the line! The CPCA was fucking *defunct*, all the anarchists just piddling around, doing nothing but smoking and drinking!"

"Like we are now," she interrupted. He ignored her.

"So *what!* Jesus Christ, I had to do something! I had to fight! I had, I had, I had to, to-"

Aleks' throat was choking up, and his eyes were glazed over more from tears than inebriation. He must've been seeing eightfold by now.

"You and me are roaches in the wall, Kyle, and yet you *spit* on me, even when I do you good!"

"I-all I did was start smoking a cigarette!"

"I failed, Kyle, I fail at everything, oh my *god*, I'm a loser."

Yeah, preach it, freak.

"No, no, n-no matter what I do - it'll always be a failure, right? Just like, all the revolutionaries, the, the men of old."

Holy shit, no, shut up, actually.

His eyes and his voice cleared, though it was obvious Aleks was no more sober than before. The grip of ideology had overtaken him again.

"Don't you see it?

"All humanity was working together, groping in the dark, for a light; some saw God, others Nation, most Capital. They all won in their own small ways, synthesizing together, waxing and waning in strength. Prime competing interests that yet embraced each other, as a father his brothers, all so proud of their children, brotherly proxy competition to be the *most* proud with their own.

"For so many reasons, all of humanity reached up their hands, with tools and hope, to the most visible lights in the sky. The sun, the moon, the planets. The great thought leaders of an era promised new ways of doing the same things. God, Nation, Capital - new names for old things, though. Our fathers and grandfathers worshiped so strongly, denied any other possibilities.

"Denied with clubs and guns and poison clouds.

"They created egregores from and for millions, Kyle."

Tears licked his cheeks, dancing on twitching muscles, reflecting the day-glo advertisements for everyone and no-one on the quiet street.

"They grabbed the planets and put price tags on them, Kyle."

He sniffed wetly and stood and walked away, his boots noisily moving grit and splashing formerly still puddle water.

Kyle blinked after him and sighed out a thick cloud of smoke.

Every fucking time.

In the blitz of noise and the clanging of her own fucking brain, wolf-girl hadn't noticed Bennett wake up to observe their disjointed fight.

"Kyle?"

He sounded almost innocent, like he didn't want to make himself a target for Kyle's surely boiling anger. Too bad she was fucking frigid; that fire was sputtering deep below in her guts, not in her heart.

"Yeah?"

"That guy, uh, Luger? He forgot his laptops."

She snorted a laugh. Burning smoke came out. She felt enough like a dragon that the ice around her innards started to thaw.

"He lives here," she muttered, waving around at the maybe-abandoned building behind her, "don't worry about it."

"Alright."

Kyle stood around and finished her stick, half-expecting her hopefully-still-a-friend to come marching in and either apologize or hit her over the head with a bat. She waited a full five minutes after she'd flicked the roasted butt into a puddle - respectfully, one outside the alleyway.

He's not coming back.

She pulled out her phone and looked at the time. 7:12 a.m.

"Hey, Bennett. You still awake?"

Shockingly enough, he responded with "yes."

"Nice. I'm hungry. You wanna get some fucking breakfast?"

"Sure. I'm fine with whatever."

She nodded and sauntered back to her bike. Kyle's ice had melted enough to expose a void of space that echoed with every thump of her heart and growled with furious need. The performative cool of her walk was over, so halfway over she started to jog back to her bike to go find something to eat.

"You mind eating off whatever I get?"

"No," the tiger replied, receding back into the depths of the pocket, "I'm fine with whatever. It'd be a waste to get me a whole meal."

"Cool. Thanks."

She slapped the kickstand up with her heel and fastened her vest pockets - though her hands reached for the cigs first, she mentally slapped them to secure Bennett instead - and seated herself as comfortably as she could. She took one last look to make sure Aleks wasn't running in to assault or assuage her.

A little bit of blood had come off her sneaker in the damp alleyway. She could see the fading pattern from her pacing and shifting that disappeared as past-her returned to the bike.

Kyle looked at her shoe, saw only a normal amount of residue, turned her head up, saw no friend returning, and felt an impossible, wistful emotion; tracked in mud and left with spite.

She revved the bike and backed out of the alley instead of driving through it. She didn't need sunglasses, despite driving directly at the blurry sun behind the world's veil.

God, I'm hungry.

3

"Communist" Burgers and Fries

7:48 a.m.

The encompassing everything-nothing drone of the city hid the approach of a food cart. Kyle and Bennett both perked their ears nearly simultaneously when they heard the screech of the push-powered music player turn on just a few dozen feet from them. That unearthly wail carried a sorrowful, unsettling history to it, the bow on the package of worn-down edges and wheels that wobbled on a bent axle that had to have been in service before the goddamn Yew-Ess broke up.

Kyle wrinkled her muzzle at the sudden waft of eggs and spicy peppers. Her stomach nearly leapt out of her abdomen with a growl that could be heard well above the tinny cry of the food cart.

"I'd offer my services," Bennett started; his voice was raised to be heard over the passing vendor, but still carried the same taunting lilt as the middle of the night. He didn't get the chance to finish.

"Can it, prick. I'm hungry, not horny."

"Same thing, different holes."

Kyle's lips twitched inscrutably.

Philosopher's got me there.

The sound blaring from the cart stopped abruptly as the owner stopped to re-align their grip. They looked just as ancient as their shop, wrinkles as deep as a knuckle on their heavily tanned face, their wisty gray hair held out of their eyes by a headband with text Kyle couldn't read; what few syllables she rolled over in her mind sounded Dutch or German or something.

"Why not get breakfast from one of the few remaining ethical sources?"

"I would," Kyle returned, "but the only money I have is for cigs."

"So... *how* are we getting breakfast?"

Wolf-girl's confidence flagged. While Bennett's tone wasn't accusatory, it shone a burning spotlight on just how out of the question what she was about to say was.

"You know. Take it."

"Oh. Steal it?"

"Yes." Then she continued, to both cut him off and leap forward in the conversation;

"I'm like Robin Hood, because I'm poor as shit and I don't steal from street vendors."

"Are - is this why we've been staking out a McDonalds?"

"That's right," Kyle shouted, suddenly leaping to her feet. She could feel the faintest little kicks in her denim pocket as the tiger grabbed onto the button in front for stability in the lurch.

"Well, fuck it, then, jeez. Just don't jump again."

"Yeah yeah, shrimp."

Kyle couldn't stop herself from letting her tongue flick out from her lips, an automatic sass to the sasser she was leashed to for the indefinite future. She stuffed her hands in her pockets, skip-jogged along the sidewalk, and then across the moderately busy street the moment there was a clearing in the buses and cars. The moment she could reach the crosswalk, she punched the button with the heel of her hand, and bounced from heel to heel as it beeped once every two seconds, on repeat.

"You sure got spry the moment food became a reality," Bennett chimed.

"Call it a sunrise second wind. You know how slime time goes."

"How - what?"

"Oh, it's a... it's a Kyle-ism. It's-"

The crosswalk turned from the orange upturned hand to the side-to-side walking stick figure and wheelchair stick figure. Red lights for everyone but her.

"-I'll tell you later."

Ten years ago, shortly after Kyle had moved to the city, they had torn down most of the old crosswalk signs and added more 'accessibility-minded' displays. At the same time, they programmed an approximate 85% to be five seconds shorter. Unless you were with a crowd, it was prudent to rush, and so she made an effort to get to the other side well before the orange timer came back up.

Kyle noticed, as her shoes hit the concrete bordering the asphalt, that her tongue was still out, and her ears were ringing. There was a second of feral glee, like she'd just stuck her head out a window while her good buddy Bennett drove her to the park.

"Your legs are long enough," he groaned, peeking cautiously upward, "you don't have to dead fucking sprint across the hill, Kyle."

"Sorry not sorry, I'm fucking starving."

She kept her tongue out, adding a cruel snicker that she knew he could feel more than hear, a rumble from the chest he was stuck to.

"Then, by all means, take us in. Christ."

"Yeah, yeah."

Their interests aligned yet again, they both turned to face the only clean and new-looking thing on the street. A centuries-old institution, ironically enough; Mc-fucking-Donalds, the only corporation that absolutely refused to die, humbly accepting any and all stipulations in every nation, state, region, clique, warlord territory, or whatever else - all in the name of visibility, profit, and the most standard fucking food you can buy, worldwide.

The entrance on the side with the bus stop was a lot more packed than the one the two stood in front of, but they still had to shift to the side to let out multiple people with their brown-and-red paper sacks.

Already turned, she looked back at the cart hobbling its way across the intersection, and at the person at its helm; she slow-rolled her saunter into the store proper, a little fist of guilt hanging heavily right under her lungs.

Walking in was like striding through a wall into roaring heat, either from the kitchen roiling or the bodies of the constantly coming and stopping and going crowd desperate to get anything in their bodies before (or after) their shift at the corpse mulcher or mattress incinerator or whatever. Impossible to tell as they mingled together and stood contrary to the morning cool.

Said crowd hung toward the other entrance, and no head rose to look in the two's direction, even as Kyle towered over every other patron there.

Someone in the counter corner, obscured by the cross-section of modern Canadian society, shouted "ORDER UP!" and a list of numbers, and two people with soot on their outfits and heavy masks hanging around their necks put away their phones. They were out of the restaurant faster than they could say 'Thank You! Come Again.'

"You ever think we ought to say thanks to the staff more?" Bennett asked.

Kyle turned her neck to look at him fully, with both eyes, instead of the corner of one. An uncomfortably shifting splotch of striped orange and black. He smelled like sweat, cigarette smoke, crusty clothes, with a fruity hint of disinfectant. Only the last was his own contribution.

No, because they all have pensions and are considered heroes of the state.

Kyle slid her bottom lip over her top in thought; stills from news casts of fast food workers wearing communist lapels and gleefully talking about retiring early after forty years of serving Canadian workers and international comrades alike danced through her mind in a lightning slideshow.

She turned her head away and began to walk into the waiting crowd.

"I don't talk politics when I'm hungry."

"Pol-what? Kyle half an hour ago you were in the thick of it with-"

"He was talking, I was smoking."

Bennett snorted incredulously, his last intentional noise before being carried with her into the diverse milieu.

It was a truly representative slice of the Vancouver-proper pie. With her head and shoulders literally above the rest of the crowd, Kyle got a fantastic look at the spread. There was a cute couple of faceless drone-types, one chrome and leather on a leash, the other stout and red and mostly hidden by the crowd; three emo-revival-revival-revival furries, providing most of the indistinguishable murmur filling the air; a dozen tired-looking workers with zero cosmetic alterations; a floating orb with its receipt tacked with a magnet to their probable 'forehead'; two well-dressed government apparatchiks, one full-height, the other cross-legged and Bennett-sized on their shoulder; and some Conan-looking fucker with more steroids and breast meat than the discount aisle at the butcher, complete with a sword in its scabbard over their shoulder.

I just gotta fuck with this person.

Kyle edged closer to the wide-not-tall giant in question, lips pulled back over fangs in a wide, goofy, *probably* intimidating grin.

"Hey dude."

They looked at her like someone might look at a stoplight on red. She continued;

"Nice sword. You larp?"

"No," they rumbled, their voice thick and guttural, "I use it."

"Vigilante shit?"

Kyle noticed Bennett waving an arm, and turned her eyes down again to affirm he was, in fact, telling her to cut it the fuck out. Too late. The vigilante answered.

"Yes. I kill people."

Bennett clamped his palms together, literally pleading.

I say, "Yeah, for how long?" and they get angrier. I insult them. "We always come back, pussy-ass." They open their eyes wide and cut me in half. I feel so fucking smug for the split second I'm alive while the walls get plastered in greasy Me.

A deep twinge of preemptive guilt.

I just need food.

Kyle placed her right palm firmly over the pocket her charge leaned out from, who was gesticulating wildly for her to shut the *fuck* up.

"Cool."

All she said. A word pretend-ignored as the living bulk of violence shifted subtly back toward the counter.

I should totally compliment their breasts.

Kyle side-stepped away instead, back into the crowd.

"Thank you for shutting up," Bennett managed to shout above the milling auditory haze.

"Welcome," she murmured back. Then, the roar of the employees;

"ORDER UP! TWO SEVENTY EIGHT, TWO EIGHTY TWO."

The two officials worked their way quickly to the counter. Kyle, a hunch bubbling between her stomach and her heart, shadowed them. When they reached the counter, the normal-height one grabbed one bag, leaving the other for another customer.

Wolf-girl didn't pause. She reached out her long arm as that sensation of burning pitch leapt up into her throat and roared like a bonfire. She grabbed the rolled-folded top of the unaccounted for bag and followed the two officials straight back around and out the door.

"Good day, comrades," the smaller one said as their ride and peer turned to walk in a direction opposite Kyle's path.

"Good day," Bennett and Kyle said together, their voices wary and tone rising. Almost a question instead of the intended greeting and good-bye.

The tiger looked up at the coyote, and she down at him, and they both pushed their lips together and snickered.

"You're cool as ice when you have to be, Kyle. Your heartbeat only rose *slightly* above the redline."

She laughed in return, a gutteral choke of truly vented emotion. Hours of fucking stress and mystery dissipated in an ear-ringing bark of sinister glee.

"Yeah, well, it's not like dying young is a problem anymore."

The crosswalk turned white. The bag in her hand crinkled loudly as she jogged across again, and she continued;

"It's all in the performance, bud. Emotions might as well just be what you say instead of what you feel."

"Fucked up but true, and you're a hell of an actor."

"Well-"

She paused to concentrate on the side-road she hop-crossed across to get back to her bike. As soon as they were out of reach of any marauding vehicles;

"-I managed to make you afraid of me at that party you remember that I don't. Despite you thinking my tastes are *weak*."

"Yeah," he returned, a sly lilt to his small voice, "I wasn't myself performing at *all*."

"I'm going to choose to ignore that," Kyle returned curtly, but raised her left hand to give his hair a cheeky ruffle with her thumb.

"Hey- ack!"

He recoiled, shoved on her finger, even snapped his proportionally chunky teeth at her the moment she pulled away.

"Real cat behavior, fag."

Kyle swung her leg over the bike's seat and popped open the carrying bay just below the handlebars, folded up the bag of food still unopened, and set it inside.

"What do you call that compartment? Never had a bike," Bennett inquired with utmost respect.

"A frunk."

It was the tiger's time to laugh with his full fucking chest.

"Frunk? And you call *me* faggot?"

"Yeah, I - I do!"

They both laughed, and kept laughing, even as Kyle shoved him back down her pocket with that same thumb and snapped the button to keep him safe. Kyle's smile didn't drop when she pulled onto the street, nor on the entire trip back to her apartment.

The ride home was deeply uneventful. Red light green light, a crowd of voluntarily misshapen bodies mingled with your average worker every other intersection. Once in a while Kyle would even hear a shout or a cheer in passing, a sign that some vigor had entered the peoples' collective day. It was very easy to maintain that grin until she turned left onto her home street, a row of lawns with four-story brick towers in them, and then left again into the attached garage, in all its rusted, pitted excellence.

"Bennett, do me a favor," Kyle whispered.

"Yeah, boss?" His voice was muffled by all the denim. Her ears perked up on their own to compensate, an almost painful, involuntary flex.

"Can you keep it quiet until I take you out of my pocket? I don't want the landlord knowing I brought someone over."

"Sure. I'm not even here."

"Thanks."

A click of her heel and a click of her hands and Kyle had their meal free and her bike propped up by its kickstand. The food somehow smelled even stronger, and the bottom was a mat of grease-soaked paper. Kyle tucked the bag under her arm so she could use both her hands to secure her shit.

"Landlord sucks. Won't even fix the garage door."

Her shoes crunched concrete-turned-gravel as she walked back out into the filtered sun. To the side of the garage entrance was a grimy retractable fence, like one for a pet or a toddler, but instead for thieves and homeowners. The rain-stained film stuck to her fingers as she pulled fiercely to expand it over the drive and to hitch it against the other side.

"Won't even WD-40 the fucking hinges."

Kyle paused to wipe filth off on the back of her shorts, and then;

"Sorry, fucked up that I can talk and you can't. I'll shut up."

She swore she could feel two very tiny pats, but it was impossible to be sure. Kyle mentally acknowledged the maybe-gesture, turned, and walked with sudden haste through the wide open front door. The hairs on her neck rose as she felt and heard a board under her heel moan. She increased the pace. Past the two offices right inside, to the elevator in the back, hoping nobody had-

"Kyle Orlanski!"

Like a trained dog, she about-faced and walked the few steps back to the open office door on her right, but paused just before crossing the threshold.

"Kyle, I saw you. Come on in."

In a black office chair sat the proprietor of the place, a person with a squat face and a shaved head and shoulders you could carry the world with. There were two cracked-leather chairs in front of the ancient, lacquered desk, both empty.

"I think I'm okay out here, Mx. Gillespie. Can I help you?"

Wolf-girl's volume was low, and her voice was timid. A cold blizzard of fear had laid a blanket over her mind.

"Yes, you can. You can pay your rent differential."

"Ah."

She found that her palms were pressed together and she was squeezing tight enough to hurt.

"Yes, Mx. How much do I owe?"

Gillespie turned to a clipboard on their desk, and the proverbial snow began to melt.

Why the fuck do they have a clipboard? They have a computer. Foreman-pretending prick cunt fucker, I oughta-

The landlord turned back to her, a single finger stabbed onto wrinkled sheets of paper. Their voice was low, smooth, and direct. No nonsense and no anger.

"Eighty-four dollars, Kyle. It's not a lot, but I need it as soon as you can get it to me."

Gillespie lowered their head a smidge, a slight grimace distorting their already aged and wrinkled face. Kyle thought they looked like a toad, but knew she was the fly.

"As soon as possible," they continued, a touch of gravel in their throat.

The snow piled back up.

"Yes, Mx. I'll try to get you something tonight."

The landlord nodded, then motioned to the side with their head and eyes. 'Get going.'

Don't gotta tell me twice.

Kyle sort-of-not-really waved with the back of her hand, turned immediately, and quietly jogged to the back of the short hallway to call the elevator. She barely dared to breathe until it clicked into the floor and the solid doors closed her off from the 'lobby'. She further her breath until the fucking clunker finished taking her and her unannounced guest up three floors.

The hallway was nothing special. Wide enough to count as a communal space. Rigid chairs and a folded-up table in the corner. Faded red carpet that grew paler the closer it was to the one single window at the far end from the elevator. A place nobody stayed unless the power was out and playing cards by candlelight with your neighbors was the only thing to do.

Dust danced in the morning light in the view of that window. Kyle tried not to think of the years she inhaled every day she came and went. Her room was the first on the right, anyway. The newest things in the building were the electronic locks, fresh outta 2025, and this one barely hitched at all as Kyle pressed her hip against it, so the radio waves or whatever off her phone let the decrepit system know to let the one true hero home. She flicked on the light and let her eyes adjust to the darkness.

"We're here, Bennett."

Wolf-girl popped the metal button to let him out, and the little tiger cautiously leaned forward in her pocket, peaking just his head and shoulders out.

The carpet ended where the doorframe began, at Kyle's heels. A century of scuffed-up hardwood covered the one-room apartment, dirty despite her best efforts at cleaning. In one corner was a side-stacked washer-dryer combo, a little desk over it with a laptop on top and a lawn chair, years old, open and waiting. To the side of that was a kitchenette, oven and microwave and a whole three shelves over a cut-out crook of tile that looked equally exhausted, permanently stained from who knows how many residents' broth and blood.

To the left was a wall with two doors - a closet and a restroom, the latter of which was shockingly large for a one-room deal, to everyone's comfort. A couple coats and jackets hung off the hook on the back of the closet door, already visibly overstuffed.

The centerpiece of the place was an unnervingly new couch, with a coffee table, comfortingly distressed and layered up with trash and books, a good four feet away. Really, books dominated a lot of the space; the back wall was lined with bookcases that held everything from early (and now useless) 19-century political theory to old DVDs and CDs, to modern holographic memory blocks that each held a library in and of themselves - most of them bad.

Unironed pride flags, political flags, and a net with a bunch of stuffies tiled the ceiling, dimming the only ceiling light in the place's ability to un-dreary this pigsty.

"Not as bad as I thought," Bennett admitted.

"I do my least," Kyle retorted.

Toe-to-heel, she pulled off her shoes with her feet by the door. The laces were well loose enough by this point to minimize the work. She kept her socks on to preserve at least an echo of the pressure-comfort that her shoes had provided - Kyle had been awake and on her feet for four hours before the day had even begun.

She reached up and plucked Bennett out with care between her fingers with her right hand, and carelessly chucked her phone onto the couch with her left. She leaned forward at the waist, balance assistance from her tail, and placed her charge down on a pillow at the opposite end. Her sleeping pillow. Hands free, she grabbed the bag of food and whipped it to land upright on the coffee table, which she then dragged closer to the couch-bed by hooking one foot around one leg.

"Ow, my fucking ears," Bennett grumbled, deadpan.

Kyle had kept her ears flat to her head the entire time she was home to keep from scraping them against the ceiling or her flags. She bared her fangs at him in a genuinely malicious smile.

"Yeah, sorry. Won't happen again."

She stood back to her full height, pulled the cig carton out of her vest pocket, and dropped it right next to the oily bag of stolen food.

"I'm gonna go change. I bet I'm covered in blood and shit I can't see from the car wreck."

"Alright bud," Bennett mumbled, putting his hands behind his head and laying out on her pillow, "I'll see you in a minute."

"Not scared of seeing me naked, fag?" Her grin grew.

"I've seen you more naked than you can imagine. Hope you got that ulcer fixed."

Hah. Fuck you.

A seconds-long pause. She exhaled through her nose, turned, and strode to the restroom.

"Hah. Fuck you."

Shit, it sounded way more stilted like that.

Bennett only snickered.

Kyle wanted to slam the bathroom door behind her dramatically, but didn't want to break both it and the full-length mirror glued to it, and frankly didn't really care enough anyway. Wolf-girl vigorously pulled her jacket and her t-shirt over her head, unconcerned by the jingling buttons and pins on their way to hit the floor at her feet. Her bra followed, as did her cut-up shorts and what remained of her leggings, and finally, her panties and her socks. She was naked in seconds, free to look at herself, nude and perfect, in that mirror.

Kyle was tall - a monstrous seven-foot-eight-inches of lanky muscle, broad shoulders and long limbs. Her feet had four toes, two bigger middle ones, two smaller outer ones on each. Still plantigrade, just a slight nonhuman touch. She had the normal quantity of five fingers on each hand, though, powerful and gnarled-looking from working and fighting, even after all the bougie chromosome therapies and horrible diets and plastic surgeries to make her look like this. One of those furry fuckers, coyote-style. The height was hers, though.

Au naturale, fuckers.

Her hair was short-long, hanging over one side, limp by weight but with enough life that she could flip it any which way. It was all bangs and top-scruff, nothing in the back, but with overly long sideburns that frayed out as soon as they passed where her jawbones hinged. It was painted bright, bright red, with a streak of white that always seemed to cross right where one of her eyes was hidden beneath the mat.

Her fur was black. So black. Jet black began to touch on how black, but like an iceberg peeking out from the water. So black her black denim would look gray on her. So black that if she unfocused her eyes, she stopped being able to see the details of her own body. No snout definition looking straight on, no contours and shapes, subtle gradients of color or distinction in muscle groups or bones, however prominent. Like someone poured ink on the invisible woman and gave her a punk jacket.

Her fur was one of the few things Kyle really loved about herself. The joy showed in the ivory whites of fangs lining a long mouth when she smiled. Scary shit. Rip-out-your-throat shit.
Just made her happier.

It was enough to nearly buoy her when she saw her flaccid cock and balls, skin dyed black to match her fur, but not nearly enough. They stood out, not in a way she liked. She couldn't imagine getting rid of one of the last things tethering her to...

Someday.

She looked up at her breasts. At least those were nice, round and heavy - for someone about half her height. The nipples were black, too.

Kyle knelt down and balled up all of her clothes, then walked back out of the restroom, a refreshed bounce to her gait. She chucked the wad over to the corner with the washer/dryer like the billions of people who lived alone have done throughout history, and immediately turned on her heel to the closet.

She felt like something special.

Wolf-girl shoved the closet open with the side of her foot and dug through the tightly packed shirts hung above the low cabinets full of lingerie, looking for something she really really felt. If she was gonna be up another who knows how long, she'd better - *Ah, perfect.*

She pulled out a fantastically well-maintained black tank top, hemmed manually around the arms and neck and bottom, and well-adorned with a cut-out black-and-white photo of late Italian politician Something Something Marcus, asshole fascist (later rebranded 'New Nationalist') and high-profile assassination 'victim.' It was hard to tell after a hundred or so washes, but his monochrome brains spilled out along the cut-out street, while a disembodied arm of the infamously never-caught assassin loomed over the body.

This was one of her favorite shirts. It never failed to draw a dirty look when she went too close to Quayside. She balled it up and chucked it onto the couch, then threw a pair of black jeans (also manually red-hemmed) and boot socks after it.

"You almost done, then?" Bennett shouted. His small voice barely carried the eight feet.

"Yeah, just about," Kyle returned, pulling a bra over her head, and then tight panties to compress her shame. She closed the closet with her left hand, and snatched her favorite jacket off the hook. She threw it onto the pile, then thundered in a jog over to the crooked table and her waiting tiger.

"Let's fucking eat," she rumbled, face all grin.

She imagined Bennett could barely see her as anything other than a familiar black blob of malicious intent in her home's low light. Almost like the fast food bag levitated instead of her picking it up. She enjoyed the rough crinkles as she finally popped the top, and the burst of smell from shockingly still-fresh food came up to hit her augmented animal senses.

"Shit, it's a double cheeseburger and fries. Could you ask for better?"

"Plate me up, big girl. Don't leave a boy to starve."

Kyle scooped up the burger easily in one hand, placed it to her side, and then picked up the carton of fries and placed it on top of that. She dove back into the salty bottom of the bag and fished around for a napkin that wasn't totally soaked through with grease.

"What was up with that freak with the sword, anyway?" Small talk while she pulled out a half-ruined piece of paper and tore off the dry part.

"I dunno," Bennett returned. He stood up on the pillow and awkwardly walked across it, flumping back down where it shoved up against the couch's armrest. "But I really wasn't about going for another few months of memory lack."

"That's fair. Bet you deal with that a lot, with your preferences."

Kyle opened the burger wrapper. She didn't bother to check what was on it, given it was stolen and she would eat a used fucking sock at this point. She turned it over once or twice, found the spot where the meat and condiments ran right to the bun's edge, pinched, and tore off the smallest bit she could manage with her huge fingers. She held it over the sack's top, squeezed out the excess juice, and then placed that little flat nugget on a corner of that torn-off napkin.

"A little bit. I think my longest was four months, after some asshole stomped me to death and neglected to take the DNA smudge back in for... well, I just said how long."

Kyle bit the ends off a single, short french fry, and spat the crunchy nubs into the sack with the rest of the wet trash. She caught Bennett's eyes staring at her.

"My mom used to do this for me," she explained, "when I was a baby. After a tooth surgery. Get rid of the useless hard bits so you can just eat the good bits."

"That's pretty smart," he returned quietly.

One fry, one squished bit off the burger. She carefully placed that shred of a napkin with his feast right in front of him, and he dug in. It was basically a burger the size of his head, anyway.

Kyle dug into hers, too. With how huge she was, it didn't take more than a few bites to disappear the entire thing, and the fries went in one mouthful, too.

"Careful you don't get heartburn," the tiger added between mouthfuls, well after she'd finished.

"That's your job," she snickered back.

Her ears twitched when he clicked his tongue, and she choked back what would've been the greasiest, nastiest cough-laugh of her life.

Gotcha, bitch.

Kyle sat on the floor and pulled her outfit from the wad one piece at a time. Socks, jeans, tank top, jacket. Oh, that jacket. It'd seen so much, been cared for so well. Patches all over, red and black and white; she liked to pretend she was a pacifist anarchist, but the scars under her knuckle fur and her leather-tough palms said otherwise. She'd designed the back patch herself, got a local friend from another time to make it and print it. The words FUCK and TEETH, vertical, with a dog's jaws parted in a bark and a cigarette on the bottom 'lip.' If there was anything she felt defined her, it was *this*.

"Enjoy your meal. I'm gonna head out and figure out some shit. I bet you still wanna sleep your recomb off."

Bennett nodded, giving one thumbs-up that tracked her as she stood back to her full height. She reached one hand down and pulled the crumpled-up blanket she always slept with up to the pillow, above him, and then folded it over next to him. Consideration for when he was done eating.

"I'll be back... sometime."

Kyle snatched up her phone and cigarettes, thumped over to the door, grabbed her heavy leather boots, and pulled those on standing, one foot at a time. The last piece of the puzzle. Like power could fully surge through her with everything in place.

I feel like Voltron.

The sensation of being a complete neek quickly brushed that aside. She didn't turn back as she reached for the doorknob. Her voice was low with totally self-isolated embarrassment.

"Yeah, later, tiger."

Kyle pulled the door open and slipped out into the hallway, hoping that the last thing he saw was her back patch, the most evocative performance of Her. A little rivulet of anxiety ran from her chest to her stomach until she heard the lock re-engage, more for his sake than any of her stuff.

Nobody bothered Kyle on her way out. No sass from her pocket, no calls from the office. When she reached up to fasten the pocket for Bennett's safety, her hands felt no lump, and already her newly learned consideration was useless.

Wolf-girl raised her shoulders and lowered her head and drove off that residential street and onto a bustling highway. The world was alive again.

But, Kyle was alone.

4

Illmagination

9:04 a.m.

Kyle flicked between two tabs on the web browser on her phone with her thumb. The official webpage of Circus and Hell, and a nearly-defunct but open-source map website. Her eyes glazed over as she let herself disappear into the ritual, let her thoughts drift on the currents so she could half-sleep, standing up. Standing next to one of the support poles on the New Lion's Gate Bridge, who-knows-how-many-meters above the archaeologically rich and treacherous fjord. The breeze roared against her and beat her ears with sound-muffling force.

Somewhere behind her, where the horizon squashed her perception of all of creation, the former Port Moody was drowned beneath the additional 1.2% of water runoff from former ice caps and glaciers. It was a great place for amateur divers to look for vintage-style shit and then drown when they got sucked into a decrepit, collapsing basement.

At her feet, massive ocean-tankers and landed starries played the world's slowest game of chicken to get in line for the Quayside ports, while in the far forward distance, several more of the latter burned countless tons of fuel from Jupiter and Titan's inexhaustible supply to hit the salty water with little more than a minor wave. The ocean sizzled audibly, even from where she stood, from the heat of re-entry ship bellies.

Kyle pulled once more on her cigarette, but received only the bitter taste of the filter beginning to smolder. She flicked the butt out into the endless blue, and, for once, her inner dialogue was intentional.

I love this city, actually.

It was easy for her to picture the currents of supplies as food. Goods from overseas and materials from the solar system arrived in the port, mouthfuls at a time. Dispersed there, like a maw chewing them into bits, swallowing them down to distribution centers, and then pumping them all over the body. Every inch of the bloated city, from the highest skyscrapers, to the farthest goddamn reaches that bled into protected forests.

Like someone's still-breathing corpse, open-wounded and bleeding in a ditch.

The ditch is the quay.

Kyle fished for another cigarette, then mentally slapped her hand away. She distracted herself by letting her mind wander back to the stream of thought.

This body was wounded. The city had swollen with an influx of over sixty million people, climate and war refugees stretching the ability for the government to handle. The US was gone, and a few dozen statelets clung to the Canadian border, fighting meager wars on each other with the modern-time equivalent of sticks and stones.

Every wound had its own infection, and this body's blight of choice was a mixed bag of capitalist realists and New Nationalists. The former had terminally controlled this body like a fucking cordeceps, well before the aesthetic revolution; the latter, while festering at the edges, had never managed a serious in-road into the rest of the city. They usually stayed by the water, in dank abandoned buildings half-submerged in seawater. Mould amongst mould.

For decades, it hadn't felt safe to be yourself on any given street corner. Action begets reaction, and a century of aesthetic posturing by the feds and millions of 'outsiders' nearly had the seaboard in blood caught on brown uniforms. Things were too good, though - everyone had food, water, shelter. The sparks had nothing to catch on. The mould stayed in their hovels. Culture had time to flourish in this new world.

A ship passed below where Kyle stood, still flicking between the two tabs on her phone. White-tipped waves rolled off the prow and shattered against the concrete and metal bridge support into whirlpool chaos. Nothing but the boat moved the boat. It was louder than the whipping breeze. Her leathery finger pad left an oily slick on the touch screen.

Culture, itself, was a reaction - just not reactionary, in the fashy brownshirt kinda way. Mostly. Techbros brought their money and their stables of copyright that the - finger quotes - *revolutionary* Canadian feds sternly decried but accepted anyway. By that time, all the chromosomal therapy and advanced prosthetics had become vogue, but imagination had been stifled by the underdeveloped empathic routes of cis men that thought the height of body expression was having their skin change color based on their mood.

That and the base necessity of providing mass-produced limbs and organs for the average industrial worker in a post-death world.

The reaction was all the shit furries and posthuman queers were on even before the collapse of Pax - *hah.* - Americana and the sudden shakeup of moral and artistic standards. Multiple limbs, bodies the size of dolls, ants, microbes, or likewise upwards. Mangling the previously perceived laws of physics with body parts physically dislocated from totally designer bodies. Sexual appeals completely divorced from biology.

Finally, the post-queer reality, joined at the hip, consensually, with post-human life. Everybody fucks and nobody even knows what it looks like, unless you're *in* it. And to get *in* it, you gotta find a place where freaks like you are the norm, where freaks like you can grow and spread your bloody wings to lash the world, screaming and nutting, into your own image.

That's where The Circus and Hell came in. The last place Kyle knew Bennett had been, and the single, only lead she had to close out this fucking mystery.

Kinda wanna bust a rope, too.

On her hierarchy of needs, cumming was just above cigarettes and being ignored by the cops.

Kyle stepped back from the edge of the bridge nearly the same moment the ship finally passed under. She had a different immediate destination in mind, though - she was almost out of death (as if) sticks, and the SkyTrain station was just past the other end of the bridge. Cheap, efficient, above-ground rapid transit that created the public-use arteries for the entire city. Kyle clicked her tongue as she swept her left leg over her bike, parked on the pedestrian walkway she'd stood on.

Still on the body metaphors. Get over it.

Wolf-girl turned the motor over and started down the narrow pathway, ignoring the not-too-surprised looks of the one or two actual pedestrians that stood to the side to let her by.

Each of the stations were elevated, obviously, since the trains had to be. Most of the business was outside of the actual terminal areas, but a few of the newer stops had allowed small pop-up stalls to exist up in the corners by the tracks. They sold exactly what you'd expect, and exactly what she needed - coffee and cigarettes. A mote of misplaced pride swelled up in her chest.

Feel damn well like a professional.

A wry little chuckle disappeared in the thrashing wind, and she disappeared into traffic as the bridge hit land and the low dividing rail ended. A honk cut above the breeze, but she paid it just as little mind.

The wind died down the moment Kyle drove back into the protective sheath of tall buildings on artificial bedrock. The artificial stillness of buildings along zig-zag roads tied the bow on the mini-neighborhood of new-new storefronts facing away from the sea. Down their intermittent alleys could just barely be seen the tops of skyscrapers that still existed halfway under water, colored slightly green with moss and metal patina.

Wolf-girl took a left at the end of that street, back to the real stores that had existed for decades and people actually using the sidewalks. Down a road that wasn't just a paint job for property values, where the train station, a parking lot, and several lovely, storied businesses resided in a long, straight row. The sound of departing trains overhead mingled with the wash of the sea a half-kilometer away.

Kyle eased off the gas and slid into an open parking spot, close as she could manage to one of the building's walls. Normally she'd have puttered around for an empty lot or just left it on the sidewalk, but the dual miracles of 'free parking all day' and open spaces helped her ignore her primal impulse to annoy people. She flipped the kickstand out and hopped onto the pavement with one practiced swing of her body, then walked back to the sidewalk, toward the station.

The street she strolled down, toward the station, had once jockeyed with a few other areas to draw the attraction of the Circus and Hell, actually. Kyle had read that on the website just a bit ago. You could tell the scars of that failed investment lingered in the over-saturation of fucky storefronts with faded signs and faded interiors visible through their front windows.

C&H never stays in one place more than a few years. Maybe they'll get their turn here.

There weren't any buildings big enough to actually host the nomadic fuck-parade, but there was always the opportunity for low-key rest years, open air affairs that would benefit from a plethora of small businesses to include in the slow-burn hedonism. Most of them Kyle ignored, but a few familiar labels plastered across one store's A-stand caught her eye. She grinned; she had time to meander and gawk. Her heavy boots creaked as she backed up to take it in.

A neon sign, turned off but still slightly colored by burnt-in gas, labeled the place "Bigguns." An obvious one-kink stop that got relatively little traffic, by the way the sign looked like it hadn't been updated in a few years. Maybe even a decade or more. It looked the way a last-decade government poster looked, behind the times even when produced, but still authoritative and timeless. This place had lasted, even if its offerings were archaic.

Kyle looked through the dusty window at the fresh red curtain and the sun-bleached covers of vintage blu-rays of the commercial industry's first forays into her subset of mildly fucked-up kink. Dino-Woman 3D, an absolute garbage-fire thirty minutes that turned on exactly fifteen people she knew online. Mommy Vore Mouth, a back-alley offering in red states of the old Yew-Ess, considered "degenerate media" by some and "kind of fucked up" by the target audience. Wilma City-Stomper, released the same year that same country collapsed, the last filmographic creation by the Walmart family. Notable for the Walmart featured in the film itself not actually being destroyed.

She smiled a little. As corny as it was, that last one was fun. They even had tiny little squibs for the crowd scenes. Already had a copy or two at home, though.

If they had wall-to-wall videos behind the curtain, like she imagined, there were probably some gems that she'd love to have. Her eyes half-lidded, and she let her mind wander again.

The smell of dust as she pulls out a copy of Godzilla 2100, where those two furry macro nuts paid Toho to have their shitty one-color fursonas added in post. The creak of floorboards that made her neck fur rise; she didn't wanna bother the clerk. Fucker's probably taking a nap. So much media that was never meant to be made, some of it even high-quality. She wanted to rip it all down and run out with it all, save it somewhere it could be appreciated for the lovable penis-pumping schlock it was.

Kyle inhaled the fresh air deeply, stepped to the side of the A-sign, and walked on to her destination. She didn't have a few hours to blow browsing stuff she could barely jerk it to. She had fags and coffee to get.

It was unusually quiet surrounding the station. Traffic was at a usual minimum, since the people using Canada's finest transit system weren't exactly known for car ownership, but she expected at least a few people coming and going to and from the sex shops and fast food joints right across the street from the turnstiles. Barely anyone wanted a double-double or a brand new Vibra-Strap from - and she squinted to read this on the sign - "Whip-Its Emporium."

There's no way they have whippits there. Way too corpo.

Kyle passed by the thin crowd of fast food workers on their first break, but cut it close; she wanted a tiny hit of exhaled nicotine that she could inhale and keep her walking for a few more steps. She didn't even know if it fucking worked like that, but the airy fresh smell of second-hand smoke put enough of a pep in her step to hop-jog straight across the street, over the turnstile, and then up the polished-up and worn-down steps, two at a time, to the platform proper.

Here was the crowd. A slice of life, much like the restaurant she'd taken her breakfast from, all waiting in their milling and disjointed mass for a train to screech up to take them where they had to go. Nobody had time for shopping before noon.

Kyle's eyes snapped to the right, to the over-busy street cart parked in the corner. It had it all; holo-sticks and USB sticks and printed newspapers, print magazines and their contemporaries on digital media as well; bags of snacks, cartons of cigs, and a bunch of styrofoam cups in an upside-down stack next to the coffee maker. A bald, tall, and rail-thin clerk flipped through one of the magazines, their back to the world.

Kyle wasted no time sauntering up to the open window to hunch down and be seen.

"Hey. Pack of Lucky Strikes if you got 'em. You still selling coffee?"

They turned around, their stool creaking in its age. The clerk grabbed a cup as they spoke, voice thin.

"Got the cigs. Got dregs. That good enough for you?"

"That's good enough to keep me standing."

"Good enough t'pay for, then."

With one spidery hand, the clerk held the cup up to the spout and pushed down the lever to let the bitter water flow. With the other, she put the card reader on the counter between them, ruffling the pages of their magazine.

"Right."

Kyle pulled out her phone and pressed its ass to the machine. It immediately beeped, and she put her phone away with the same swiftness.

Somewhere, her father's credit card gained a $4.50 charge from an unknown source that he'd probably never notice.

The clerk set the cup on the counter, bent down, rustled up a pack of cigarettes, and placed it by the cup's side with a pleasing, solid, plastic thump.

"Come again sometime," they muttered, giving a slightly cordial nod.

"Hope not," Kyle returned, scooping up her goods.

The clerk snickered, picked up their magazine, and continued their idle reading.

Kyle turned from the stall toward the tracks, then to the people waiting. A typical crowd, milling in place, dispersed around for, ostensibly, mutual privacy, whatever the fuck that mattered. In a deft balancing act, wolf-girl used her left hand, holding her coffee cup, to pull the crumpled, nearly-empty pack from her vest pocket, and then slid in the new one with her right. In the same motion as taking a sip of bitter energy, she reached in and plucked the three remaining sticks out and slid them in bare beside their replacement. Coffee tasted like burnt garbage, but that's exactly what she needed.

She took the now totally empty pack and balled it up in her right fist. Crushing laminated paper was a soothing ritual in a way, taking something useless and making it even more so. Without anything but hot-ass bean water to distract her, she looked back to the crowd. Standing out among them all that morning were three pup play pals; one dom, two subs, by the look of it.

The big one, holding the other twos' leashes, had at least three other empty ones in their other hand. Kyle took unnecessary interest, furrowed her brows, and hid her thoughts behind another sip.

Is there a parade or something going on later?

Also, the two subs were wearing blindfolds. An impressive trust exercise, especially as the dom gently nudged the shorter sub closer to the tracks. A girlish squawk filled the air as that shorty, some scaly-looking nerd with a lizard snout and stubby horns, nearly tripped over the blind-accessible bright yellow bump line at the edge.

Everyone turned their head toward the oncoming train as they could see it crest the treeline around the bend, mostly from the gentle gleam of its reflective front catching the faded sun. The squeal of metal wheels on the track carried on the wind, growing louder every moment. Kyle side-eyed the puppies in the corner, restless and awkward.

C'mon, be gentle with 'em. Don't wanna cause an accident.

Ignorance is bliss, but her eyes caught their movements. The dom's hands unlatching the scaly's leash. Swiftly undoing the blindfold of the other. Weird. Weird shit. Don't care. Don't wanna know. She focused on the ball of crumpled-up paper in her hand and impulsively flicked it onto the tracks. The tip of the train entered the station.

A loud yelp. Everyone turned from the roar of the metro sliding past them in slow motion. Kyle got to see, for just a moment, the blindfolded bottom, still making the cute little puppy-hands, free-falling in front of the moving train.

Wolf-girl's ears flattened to her head. She didn't know if she heard the *thunk* over the honking of the horn and the premature screeching of clenched brakes. It pictured itself in her mind, *Stop, please don't-*

The smack of flesh at a hundred miles an hour,

STOP,

      and the rolling crack of bone,

         PLEASE STOP,

            and *the* cinematic *splatter* of *hot*

              red

                blood.

Kyle chucked her coffee into the nearby bin, a furious, instinctual action that coincided with the overwhelming, uncomfortable clench of abdominal muscles keeping down bile and breakfast. She took in a high-chested breath and rolled her jaw back, exhaling harshly down over her bottom lip in an attempt to keep everything down.

"Ah, fuck. That'll give me a headache," the shopkeep shouted. "You not from around here, girl? Try not to lose your lunch, it'll be over in a few minutes."

Kyle shot them a nasty stare, a few seconds of relief from the gnarled bite of her own immature trauma.

Everyone else on the platform booed or groaned. Small, pithy complaints of being late for work or for an appointment filtered through the on-off screech of the train's horn. The door opened, and people walked out to shout or shrug at the dom, who, for their part, shamelessly backed against the wall to start fondling themself. They gave a thumbs-up to a few people who clapped and laughed and walked on.

The station's speakers cut through the constant honk; "Attention Comrades, the train will be stopped momentarily due to mechanical problems. Thank you for your patience."

God I'm a fucking dweeb, fuck, this is normal, this is okay, just supposed to be annoying.

Kyle anxiously scanned the crowd for someone, anyone, who hadn't just immediately gone back to looking at their phone or newspaper or just stepped onto the train to wait out the janitorial recovery efforts. A few people were more perturbed by events, but she was by *far* and away the most *touched*.

The one who looked most shocked, besides her, must've been some country boy. You could make the assumption with his bowl haircut and body that looked like lean muscle-wrapped rebar, wearing an outfit way out of his class. One hand on his face, the other limply holding onto a briefcase that rattled ever so slightly with his involuntary shake of fear. Wolf-girl thundered over on steps loud enough to hear, for her own sake, above the staccato beep of the stopped tracks.

Without ceremony, she placed her wrist on his far shoulder, and he snapped out of his stupor to twist and look her in the face, towering a full fucking foot and a half over him. His eyes widened in renewed terror.

"You're not from around here, huh?"

God, I'm slick.

Kyle noticed she couldn't notice her nausea anymore. Too focused on this shaking little dude from another world.

"N..no, I, uh, uh, I,"

His voice was about as stable as his presumed mental state.

"Calm down, Jethro," she continued, placing one palm against his chest.

Is that silk?

"Sorry, I'm - not from around here," he agreed. "Not used to casual death and talking dogs."

"You're awfully well-dressed for a country boy." She couldn't stop herself from fingering glossy buttons and ruffling that - *It IS silk* - much to his growing disdain.

"Are you going to mug m-me?"

Kyle snorted, and she must have looked *very* scary doing so, because he visibly shrank from her.

"I only steal from corpses, corps, and cops. Five-finger discount doesn't apply to people who don't have anything they can replace."

"That's good."

A pause. She could tell Country-Boy had more to say.

"I'd hate for you to steal my passport. I'd hate to be stuck... here."

He half-turned his head toward the scene rapidly progressing at the front of the train. Pupmaster Flex had finished, and was being berated by a cop who'd stepped off, a janitor, and the conductor. They both turned away the moment that the short-term memories of what'd just happened began to creep up at the corners of their mind.

"I'm... a union representative from the United Syndicates of Washington and Oregon."

Her eyebrows snapped up in surprise.

"Holy shit. Our friendly kooks to the south!"

He frowned severely. It was almost enough for Kyle to lose the smug smile on her face. Her wide shoulders tensed up on their own.

"I'm sorry we don't meet the idea of capitalist realism enough for you aesthetics-choked fr-...friends."

"Babe," Kyle wheezed, rolling her eyes up and away, "I've had enough talk from politically pure activists for one day, and it's already rolling into the second I've been awake."

"I'm surprised you get lectures at all."

"I'm surprised you about-faced so hard."

"I'm - "

He started with so much vigor that the dribbles of an aborted spittle-spray stuck to his lip. Kyle blinked. He blinked.

" - out of my element and defensive. And. Unwell, from seeing... uh, over there."

He pointed with the back of his hand and his thumb, unnecessarily.

"Why don't you just hop on the train, there? They'll get it running in a hot minute, get you where you need to go."

Kyle stroked the front of his chest, smoothing out his very nice suit that she'd ruffled with her incessant, nervous touch. Somewhere in all the mockery, the train had stopped honking.

"That quickly? After a death on the tracks?"

Wolf-girl's heart lightened a little. A buoy of glee as she got to remind herself of something at the same time she informed another. Collective comfort.

"Nobody *dies* up here, anymore. They got that recombination shit on every other corner."

He blinked, looked back over at the scene behind him - which had well ended, with just two janitors on the tracks with buckets and mops and a volunteer collecting the sub's personal belongings for later return. They were visibly finishing up, passing a cigarette back and forth.

Kyle wasn't nauseous anymore.

"Huh."

"Get on the train, you're gonna be okay. Everyone's okay. This is normal."

She patted him on his opposite shoulder, and he barely budged. All the vigor of a life of hard labor, with plenty left to give, was returning through his dissociated sheen. He looked back at Kyle, and she tilted her long snout down to meet him eye-to-eye. He couldn't be more than 25, but his face was deeply tanned and gnarled. He'd spent most of those 25 years outside, getting those raw-ass UV rays straight to his core. Made him look worldly. Handsome.

"Yeah. Thanks, uh. Comrade?"

His teeth looked like shit. Kyle's smirk grew; fucked-up fangs solidarity.

"Save your 'Comrade's for the people who eat up the aesthetics bullshit, like you said."

Aleks would eat this shit up. Probably call him a 'Statist,' ruin a blossoming heart in the ruins of some guy needing his daily nut.

"Canada's pretty weird, friend."

Kyle let go of his shoulder, reached up to her chest, pulled out one of the loose death sticks next to the pack she'd just bought, and stuck the end in her lips.

"How do you keep that in," the once-American asked.

"Don't ask. Welcome to Canada."

She could *feel* his eyes staring at her back as she walked away, something close to happy that the last view of her would be the giant 'FUCK // TEETH' patch on her jacket. That sinister comfort disappeared the moment she reached the bottom of the steps, though, as she was again alone. While she fished with her right hand for her lighter, she brought her left up to touch the pocket she'd left Bennett in for the past four hours.

She remembered The Circus and Hell.

Again, she thought; *Someone might know Bennett there. I can do something fun for once. Two birds, one stone.*

So she crossed the street, puffed her cig to help light it, passed the lonely fappers' libraries, hopped on her bike, and rode in the direction of the rest of her terrible awful very bad day.

5

The Circus, and Hell

11:31 a.m.

In a repurposed convention center, near a crowded bus stop, by an overworked major hospital flanked by two smaller clinics, surrounded by the shouting, laughing, screaming, crying, whooping masses of Vancouver's horniest, lie the center of a city. Metaphorically, at least - it was fairly south, still inside the city limits proper, but it *was* the throbbing clit of whatever culture the city was worth.

From her position past the entry barriers expropriated from the pigs, Kyle could see at least three social media and art luminaries mingling with the more chilled-out crowd outside. One of them was the Sargon to Aleks' Lugal, a pale, bespectacled hunk of a man named Osian leading a chant too muffled by the rest of the crowd to hear. At least three other people wore the same pink-and-black armbands as him.

These deep red districts, big or small, were the only places without the incessant advertising so prominent everywhere else in the city. They had their own, sure, as Osian was proving, but it wasn't the same soulless drek that was pumped across billboards that blocked out apartment owners' morning suns. No, there was too much defiance here, too many raised fists and multi-cocks and rivers of blood splashing at the feet of the revelers to properly sell something like a new cell phone to.

The only freedom is here, huh.

Kyle took a long drag on her cigarette, remembering Aleks, remembering the morning, remembering to take a mental note to never mention she'd seen Osian actually *doing* something to him. Memories for her to drown and disappear in the slurry of short-term memory overload the moment she walked through the black curtains to her right, into the hopeful early terminus of her day's events.

The ground was littered with cigarettes, and Kyle added one more, not bothering to put it out with her heel.

Somebody might want it.

All she had to do was walk into the front and ask one of the receptionists about the micro corner. Ask about Bennett, and if that failed, ask about Bennett to the other inches-tall.

Kyle hunched forward over the chest-high barrier - to others, not to her - and laced her long fingers together. She worked her jaw back and forth, sucked on her lips and her teeth with no real purpose but to satiate a ritual need.

C'mon. Get up.

She squeezed her palms together more tightly. Her eyes obeyed her anxiety instead of her will, and flicked to several points where the crowd was closest. Nobody looked at her, and that paradoxically terrible fact balled up a glut of burnt sensation between her chest and her stomach.

Someone out of sight laughed loud enough to hear above the din of hundreds. A single-note like a gunshot. Kyle winced.

C'mon. Get UP.

Kyle pushed away from the barrier with her elbows and disassociated her way into shouldering past two viciously average lesbian-lookalikes on her way into the building. Her head felt like it floated above her neck, brain inflated by a billion-trillion-quadrillion new stimuli that she would have time to take in later, after getting directions.

The receptionist desk was an electric shade of pink-not-quite-purple, or the other way around. Someone with dreadlocks and a smile a mile wide sat behind the right side of the desk, flanked by two professional-looking bouncers that towered even over Kyle. They leaned their left cheek into their left hand, from which dangled a lanyard and badge with plain "They/Them" printed in four different languages.

Kyle could tell that's what it said because she had walked straight up to the desk with zero hesitation (which she regretted) and zero control (*Ditto*). The receptionist's brilliant green eyes turned up and up to her, that smile not fading a smidge.

"Hey, lost? Need some help?"

That evident?

The bitter sting pulled Kyle back to the driver's seat of her own body.

"Yeah, a little lost. I got pre-cleared consent," she lifted and waved her sleeping phone from her pocket for a moment, "but I don't know exactly where the micro corner is."

The receptionist pulled up a tablet as thin as a razor off the table, the dark colored glow still illuminating their face well above the ability of the high ceiling lights. They looked almost like a completely normal person, except for the subtle, iridescent shimmer of - scales? - in the shifting light of their display.

"Oh! Right. Yeah, if you take a right down the hallway," they pointed with their left arm, pinky outstretched for manners' sake, "then another right, and push past some curtains, you'll find the set of booths with them. You'll have to pass through the cyber-sex block, but you'll be fine."

"To my understanding, it's all black drapes that get adjusted constantly, yeah?"

"It can be a little confusing for newcomers," they admitted through voice tone and forward body gesture.

Kyle opened her mouth to complain, say something snarky, keep up the pace and tone of the day, but she felt eyes boring into the back of her head. She wasn't the only one who needed service.

It's cool, it's like the open-planning kink shit. This is cool.

"I'll just ask someone else if I get lost, yeah?"

They smiled somehow even wider, pure, uncut glee. It was infectious. Kyle found herself standing up a little straighter in response.

"That's the spirit! Welcome to the Circus!"

"And Hell?"

Kyle wished she'd bit her tongue, expecting the social equivalent of someone pulling a fucking revolver and executing her as an example. Instead, they just snickered and pointed with their right thumb down the hallway far fewer people were milling around. There were three stretchers set up against the wall, one with visible blood stains.

"Right. Nevermind. Thanks." Kyle's response was short, and she gave a small wave before taking off in the exact opposite direction, into the maze of black fabric.

Busy as it was near the entrance, the jostling crowd petered out rapidly as everyone found their way to their desired fuckholes. After one fork in the hallway, Kyle found herself surrounded by a milling group of real chrome-domes, the kind with exposed wires laced through their skin like corset piercings, the ones with retropunk chunks of metal replacing parts of their body for the aesthetic, a whole array of electro-bio jacks embedded at the bases of their skulls.

Long, industrial-grade wires sheathed in rubber and stuck down with tape lay across the floor, not haphazardly as much as desperately. At least ten conversations were loud and close enough to clearly hear, but their combined, discordant noise made it impossible to pick out a word, even a syllable. People of all sizes and shapes strode or crawled or fluttered through the blackout curtains creating a maze of booths, and some even gave Kyle a moment's notice - she was pretty fucking tall, all things considered. They passed on immediately, though. She wasn't nearly the most *interesting* thing they'd likely seen all day long.

She thought of herself drawing eyes in a pink tutu, snorted, and scratched under her chin instead of reaching for another cigarette.

The charnel house had so many things to see, and to avoid seeing, and she couldn't help but act the tourist and turn her head to every new little stimulus. There was a visual basilisk hanging from the ceiling, and Kyle snapped her wandering eyes away as quickly as she could. That was a feature for others, not meant for her *primitive* taste. She pinched the bridge of her nose and inhaled deeply the sex-salted air, bracing against the headache that suddenly welled up behind her eyes.

Fucking guys putting brain burners out in public, christ.

It passed after a few deep breaths, pushed out by the perpetual churn of new information assaulting her barely-plastic brain. The unnatural crackle of high voltage to her side and the spike of ozone-smell helped, in their own terrifying way. Kyle kept moving.

Down the hall, to the right.

The last of the voyeurs and techsex fanatics found their places, and wolf-girl found herself walking alone, wandering through increasingly narrow and labyrinthine ad-hoc halls of black fabric. She tried to stick to the spirit of her instructions, one arm out to brush against the 'wall' to her right. She counted the booths, most of which were consistent with the staccato groans of oversized computing hardware, plugging away at something inscrutable. Visions of VR sex danced in Kyle's mind, too boring and predictable to be the truth. She just kept going;

Down the hall, to the right.

The last booth in the hall sounded completely different, only small noises that were something like metal and plastic. Tiny, tinkling. Kyle pulled open the curtain, high enough that the people inside might not notice her if it were, somehow, the wrong stall. She blinked twice and inhaled sharply the moment she realized it was *absolutely* the wrong stall.

A completely normal person was blindfolded, gagged, and strapped to a flat table by their wrists and ankles, and with further straps around their thighs and chest. They could barely flex as the nearly Kyle-height furry above them leaned in and whispered a deep-chested 'You're a good girl, you're gonna be fine,' before letting a pile of - *salt?* - drop out of their hand and onto the bound person's smooth, shaved stomach.

Then they leaned over to grab something off of the thin metal tray atop an instrument table with their black-gloved left hand, and, noticing Kyle, shot their eyebrows nearly to their three-tone mohawk.

"Oh, hey. Here to watch?"

The surprise didn't daunt them at all. They looked something like a hyena, all broad and powerful, striped fur with pink highlights. Naked, tits out, black gloves, standing just short of Kyle's exaggerated height. As they spoke, they waved what they'd picked up at her like a pointer - a fucking scalpel.

"Oh, uh. Sorry, I was looking for the, uh. Micro room."

"Oh! Yeah, yeah, that used to be right, but they moved past the curtain. Noise level and all. Just push past the drapes."

They grinned, not letting Kyle leave just yet.

"Sure you don't wanna watch?"

Kyle nervously wetted her lips, then motioned vaguely with her head to continue. The hyena leaned in and whispered to their partner;

"Hey, good girl. We've got an audience for you. Put on a show."

The bound one writhed in place, their muscles sliding powerfully under nearly fatless skin. Were anyone watching a doctor, they'd have loved to see the anatomy before its presumed defilement.

"My name's Bucks, she/they," the hyena added as she shifted her scalpel to her right hand and tilted to let Kyle get a better view. She leaned close to that little pile of grit, slightly toppled from the sub's wriggling. Carefully, she leaned one long arm around, and placed the blade just beyond it. She pressed in, and it easily slid into that perfect, pale skin, releasing a clean wave of bright red.

Kyle stared and held her breath. Bucks dragged the scalpel a few inches, opening a lengthening incision that released so much more crimson. Most of that flow landed against the pile of probably-salt, soaking up into it and coloring it like snow.

Then Bucks closed her eyes, let her tongue out, pressed it into that bloody heap, and dragged it forward over and into the incision, spreading that substance around and inside the cut with a practiced and indulgent pace.

Kyle's stomach leapt into her chest, and her balls disappeared with the same haste.

This owns so hard. What the fuck.

The sub writhed. Kyle's ears perked painfully high as the muffled screams started. Bucks leaned her elbow on the bound one's stomach, partially on the wound, and turned to grin wide at wolf-girl's shocked expression. Everything from her nose down was matted with fresh blood.

"It's just gonna be more of this for an hour. You can go when you've had enough."

God, I wish.

"I *do* actually have to get going, ahaha, but! This is really cool, and have fun! Uh! Both of you!"

Bucks extended her arm to gently tap the round heel of her scalpel against the sub's forehead. They somehow, amongst their shivering and flexing, shuddered in reaction.

"Actually, it's more like fourteen of us. Safe travels, have fun with our fellows."

Kyle stepped away from the curtain, but not before seeing Bucks reach over for a classic box of Morton's. Her balls refused to unclench until she'd found the back fabric wall the latter had mentioned; she shouldered through two layers of heavy canvas, and found herself in one long, straight hallway, with one single bend, to the right.

As she walked, she said to herself again;

Down the hall -

She hit the corner after a few long strides. To her side there was a single booth, about fifteen by fifteen feet, much more well-illuminated than the entire rest of the fucking Circus. A central table, bright white plastic, with five inches-tall figures seated around what qualified as a table for them in the middle. The micro booth for this side of the venue. One of them noticeably turned, even across the gap between her and them, and waved pleasantly.

Kyle swallowed a mouthful of spit, a normal, natural thing for anyone else; her dick pulsed firmly. The wires in her brain were crossed to hell at the sight of what she wanted.

- and to the right.

It was quiet enough that she noticed the rubber creak of her boots flexing with her steps. She rapidly grew performatively self-conscious, exaggerating her steps, raising her chin, all fun little things to put herself in the headspace of someone who wanted to fuck these five little things *up.*

Consensually, of course.

"Hey, all," Kyle mumbled as she crossed the threshold, instantly wiping away the last three seconds of pumping herself up.

A couple tiny snickers, and one welcoming smile, from that same tiny worker that had waved her over. They were another furry, thin and long, like a ferret, and slightly less anthropomorphic than the mostly disinterested fox-like sitting next to them, or Bennett back at home, or Kyle herself.

"Hey, tall, dark, and horny," they cooed. Their syrupy voice flowed through Kyle's ears and down to her heart, setting her instantly at ease. Wolf-girl felt the corners of her mouth twitch up in a momentary smile.

"Hi. Kyle, she/her."

The mustelid tilted their neck in response. "Violet, she/her too. What can I do you for?"

"I - well, uh, I have a couple questions, actually."

The fox lifted their head, both eyes covered by their bangs.

"Missing person or your first time doing this?"

Violet rolled her eyes. They looked like little designer black glass beads for tiny dolls. Kyle imagined them glistening in the last rays of light as her canine jaws closed around the ferret's head and torso and-

Kyle clenched her jaw tight to crack down on her mind. Her voice noticeably cracked in her response.

"The - ah, kind of? This guy, Bennett Quail? Got dumped in my hands when the clinic couldn't find his records."

The five all looked up from their phones and at one another. Two humans, two furries, one impossible to place cool-looking cylindrical nightmare of magnetized fractal metal sliding over themself again and again in thought.

Probably gets a lot of work being the most responsive vibrator in town.

"Rings a bell," that mechanical person vocalized, their outer rings and inner rings shifting over one another with increased fervor.

"Please tell me you can point me to his house," Kyle murmured.

"No can do, Kyle. He hung out with us for a weekend, got bored, and left."

The metal comprising their body ceased to move, and they came to a rest against the table again.

"Sorry. They were probably just a daytripper."

Kyle inhaled deeply, popping both hands out of her pockets just to lace them together on top of her greasy head. After a second of nothing poignant presenting itself to her from the creaky depths of her mind, she hissed out an exasperated sigh.

"Well, I guess I've got zilch for leads, then."

No-one spoke. Here between the curtains, it was the quietest place in the city.

"Fuck," she continued, and let her hands fall to her sides as she did, "I got nothing. Violet, you wanna fuck?"

"Sure. Beats looking at my phone until my shift's over. How much are you gonna pay?"

Kyle stepped closer to the table and placed both of her hands palm-up for the ferret to climb into. She smiled sheepishly;

"I've got five bucks and a free trip to the recomb for you."

Violet put a hand on one of wolf-girl's raised thumbs to brace herself; they both knew the size-difference song and dance.

"That's food for a week, Tee Dee Haytch. There's a private room straight down the hall from you."

Kyle stood, but kept the heels of her hands together in front of her at her waist. She was now a chariot for her hire.

"Catch you all tomorrow or the next, by the sounds of it," Violet called back to the others. A few hands rose in casual waves; this was normal. It was normal that everyone had heard Kyle say she was going to fucking kill their friend, if only for a day.

Normal like the train.

Wolf-girl tried her best not to clench her abdomen at the thought. Her stomach rose into her chest for a second in a swell of involuntary muscle as she strode from the room.

"Is it weird that I was the only customer today," Kyle asked, her voice and breath both stuck in her throat.

"While you won't be," Violet began, "it's not that busy for us, usually. Our corner always seems, ah, *underutilized*, because nearly a third of the population ate up the government's propaganda about downsizing for the resource stability and waste saving that it would entail.

"In short,"

Violet paused to laugh in her throat,

"-there's so many of us that you can usually just find someone you love to bits in your daily life and then *fuck* to bits just the same. No need to really go to the hub of all things depraved and beautiful, you know?"

Kyle lifted her spare hand, previously used to shield and support the ferret in her ride, to brush aside a curtain to the other quietest room in the city, this one completely unoccupied save for the two wildly physically different women.

"Basically, I'm a dork," Kyle muttered.

"Right on the money, Lurch."

Kyle winced. Violet hung onto her thumb a little tighter.

"Do I have that bad a gait?"

"No, you're... tall. You know, Lurch?"

"I don't get it."

"Forget about it, Mt. Fairweather."

Kyle shrugged while keeping her hands still.

Got me there.

Kyle slowly sat on the one provided couch, all pleather and plastic that creaked uncomfortably under her considerable bulk. She hooked her right heel around the base of the table in the middle of the room and dragged it closer. The walls seemed to swallow the sound.

She licked her lips; nervously or not, she couldn't tell.

"They were right, by the way. This is my first time coming here. All the other people I've done shit with were randos at parties, or assholes on the street calling me names that I pulped and jerked off about later."

"Very candid of you," Violent responded, motioning to be let onto the table. Wolf-girl nodded and raised her hands to the lacquered wood for her. The ferret began to unbutton her shirt, an evidently well-tailored polo, and continued;

"I could see you coming here often. An environment a lot less judgemental than the one out there."

"Maybe, Violet. It's a little bit different."

She looked to the door, a paranoid timefiller, then back to her fuck-meal.

"If it helps to know, most repeat customers end up working with us."

"I don't think I could. I'd rip someone's throat out."

"There'd be a place for that."

Kyle smiled. A guilty admission.

"Well."

A non-starter of a rebuttal

"C'mon and relax. Tell me what you're about while I get ready."

Violet's outer layer dropped away from her, showing off previously unnoticed curves.

"I, uh. I wanna. Eat you."

Violet reached down to her pants and popped the button on the front without even a moment's hesitation.

"Is that all?"

Kyle felt sweat bead on her brow, watching her strip. A subtle heat began to well up around her persistent half-chub.

"Yeah, that's all. I'm really into... that."

The ferret pulled her bra off, two tiny, saggy, fucking *ideal* breasts releasing heavily against her chest. The couch groaned under Kyle's nervous roil.

"Are you a chewer, Kyle? Gonna make me feel like a bit of gristle in that greasy maw of yours?"

"No. I don't - not that."

"You're more into the sensual stuff?"

Oh she wants to call me a faggot real bad.

Wolf-girl nodded. Her tail beat quietly next to her, against the pleather. Plap plap.

"Cute. Do you do any writing?"

Violet dropped her panties into the pile of clothes at her paws. She was beautiful naked, if a little unconventional. Most people didn't like the really half-and-half anthro bodies, the ones that weren't just humans with fun animal bits stuck on. She really seemed special.

"You're gonna call me the Sapphos of vore freaks, huh?"

That same broad smile from the moment they met returned.

"I like it when people flatter themselves for me."

Kyle laughed, a forced, firm, dark laugh. The other continued;

"No, no, really. You don't get how often I get people that hate themselves."

"Trust me, Violet - I hate myself plenty."

"Maybe, Kyle, but - put your hands on the table."

She did so, palms up. The naked beauty practically radiated light from her auburn fur. Kyle winced again, like she expected Violet's little paws to burn her like a lightbulb. She was warm, sure, but like the warmth of practiced care and love for hire she should've expected.

"Kyle, try to be nicer to yourself today and tomorrow, yeah? You're going to get hit with some pretty hard dom drop, I can tell."

"Always do," Kyle returned, her voice small.

"Let's get it going, then. Just pop a five back in the other room before you leave."

Kyle nodded and smiled, albeit weakly. Violet laid on her front in the coyote's palm and motioned up with one arm. The former swallowed firmly, realizing just how heavily she was salivating. She stood, braced her left hand against the table in front of her, and raised her right up to her face. The ferret pinched her fingers together, then spread them. The most obvious fucking instructions that still took a few full seconds to properly register.

Kyle opened her jaws wide, still slick with evident desire.

"Beautiful," Violet whispered, audible above the pounding in Kyle's ears.

Kyle twisted her eyes shut, huffed once, and, with a motion as simple as downing a pill, shoved her partner into her mouth.

The ferret writhed on top of wolf-girl's tongue, awkward side-to-side movements between her teeth that morphed into a forward-to-back roil.

Oh my god she's fucking my tongue holy shit

Kyle closed her jaw with a deep, shuddering exhalation. Frantically she grabbed at the buckle of her jeans, unzipping and popping the button to let her suddenly *vastly* harder cock flex out in its underwear tent. She hooked her two thumbs through that elastic and pulled it down in kind. Her raging length audibly thumped against the tabletop and scattered the micro's discarded clothes.

Violet worked her way deeper into Kyle's mouth, and the latter could feel tiny kisses against the sensitive rug of her panting tongue. She could barely feel her accelerating breath on her lips, most of it stopped by that writhing, humping body moving from her canines to her premolars, and then beyond. She felt two tiny hands on her gums, well behind the backs of her teeth.

Holy fuck holy Fuck holy fuck

It takes eight seconds for food to travel from the mouth to the stomach. One of those seconds is the most critical, the brain-fogging terror before whatever one swallowed slides past the branch in the pipe to let you breathe safely again. Kyle imagined what it would be like to be swallowed whole, for a second, as she tilted her muzzle back and forcibly clenched her throat to start dragging sweet Violet down.

One second. She could *feel* Violet's sudden writhing - there was no going back now, for either of them. Tiny legs scratched at the backs of her molars, sound-sensations tickling her tall ears. Little arms thrashed in the sensorially-muted curve of her throat, grabbing at nothing, not even tonsils. She held her breath and scrunched her muzzle, swallowing again with desperate gusto to push her partner past the squeeze and down her esophagus proper.

Kyle couldn't breathe and the timer had barely started; she grit her teeth and swallowed yet again, and Violet's lithe body was finally pulled down with a non-audible *pop*. Kyle nearly hurt her cock squeezing it so hard.

Oh fuck oh fuck this is IT-it!

Foreign sensations, ghoulish approximations of what a too-big bite of food mash feels like, all burning and fighting against muscle and fat. Except it was wriggling, writhing, clawing, and *fucking* at the smooth red flesh of Kyle's throat. Inexorably pulled down by a ring of flexing muscles past the branch - *sweet fucking air i gasp in desperately so i dont pass out when i cum* - and disappearing deeper, deeper, past her heart - *oh jesus shes so warm its so tight it hurts* - sliding down, down, down, *down*.

The wolf-girl's eyes seized and rolled up of their own accord. Violet hadn't even hit her stomach and her whole body was twitching and tensing as she struggled not to cum.

There was a sinking feeling, a relief that washed through her, some unconscious, animal emotion that underlaid her grit-teeth throat-whine desperation. Violet wasn't moving down anymore. The weight of a whole *fucking person*, thrashing about in whatever disgusting sludge that was left from her breakfast.

It had taken a little longer than eight seconds for her to hit home.

Kyle went over the edge. Feeling the ferret-girl thrash around in the swampy muck of chyme-slop was too much. It was cemented - total power. The diminishment from prey to food. Her padded grip on her cock quivered, and an electric heat spread all over her groin. She instinctively bucked into the air, her pelvis slammed against the table. Her cock flexed beyond its limits and she felt her fucking *soul* leave with her chest with the spray of nut and a soft belch that turned into simpering apologies.

"Aauuggfuck, I'm sorry, oh fuck, I'm sorry, I'm, I'm, s-sorry, ohhh fffuuuckk..."

The fun thing about stomachs is that there's no air in them. It was common knowledge in the vore scene that eating people whole, while out of vogue for *some* in the community, was the more intimate and softer style, as the 'victim' would slowly fall asleep in the warmth - supposedly it was incredibly comfortable.

Kyle gingerly let herself down onto the pleather couch, spreading a few new cracks in the upholstery when her knees gave out and she couldn't slow down her sit. Violet, likewise, settled down - more from a lack of ability than active calm. Kyle placed her hand on the outside of her stomach, slowly patting her tummy, and her partner inside.

"Thank you, Violet... thank you, I'll get you out..."

She let her eyes roll back again as she felt two tiny hands poke at her palm through the thin muscle of her abs. Her limp cock twitched, and she winced.

"...a-as soon as I can stand again."

Violet had stopped moving long before Kyle herself could stand.

True to her word, Kyle zipped up her pants and waddled on weak knees back to the room with the other downsized workers. She rolled up a five CAD bill and set it down in the one empty seat.

"Thank you," the fox with bangs said with a knowing smirk.

Bashfully, she returned the smile.

Tracing her steps back to the front was simple - go back in the vague direction she came from, and follow the people until she found the crowds. The crowds that laughed and moaned and rubbed elbows (and other parts) in the open air, and yet ignored and passed by others they had no business with. It was like a big busy family house, everyone full of a deeper sense of love than the fairly surface-level fucking.

Kind of a waste to be here.

Not even the last of the afterglow could keep her head above emotional waters. She *had* essentially wasted all her time and the last of her money coming out here, didn't even get answers for the one thing unanswered.

Could've even jerked off at home.

It was the dom-drop that Violet, sweet Violet, once a woman, now food, and soon to be a woman again, had warned her of. Kyle shouldered past someone literally nailed to a cross taking up too much of the hallway and rubbed her tummy - not with any discomfort, just a sort of wistful, parasocial longing.

An electric *snap* as loud as a gunshot caught her attention. She whipped around suddenly to one of the booths devoted to the cyberfuckers, one of whom pulled open the curtain to look at the curious and concerned mass of Vancouverites.

They pointed right at Kyle.

"You. Come check this shit out."

Yeah, whatever. Sure.

She edged through the crowd and stepped into the booth, blocking the view of what was happening inside with her hand-made back patch and legs that *did* in fact go all the way up, thank you very much.

The technician looked a little like Gollum, but with the top half of their head replaced with a square block of metal, four red, glass eyes set vertically on the right edge. They weren't naked, but had plenty of wires stuck in the back of their neck and looped out their sleeve, into the obviously experimental machine on the floor. The smell of ozone was overpowering.

"You know what this is? This is fucking *groundbreaking* tech in the geometrical sex space."

Kyle's mouth pulled to one side and her brows furrowed powerfully.

"Like, math shit?"

"Yes! I'm currently rendering this area as a fourth-dimensional still fractal with visual-neural-sexual nerve bleed-over, and *god* my clit is *hard*."

The coyote clicked her tongue, then motioned behind her with her thumb.

"Cool. Can I go?"

"No, no no no! Because you're about to see what happens when I overclock it! I'm going to be the *first person* to ever sexually view, like, with my brain, the *fifth dimension!*"

"Cool."

Kyle stepped back.

"I'm going."

The cyberfucker reached to the machine, pushed through a literal mat of tiny wires, and pulled down on a comically oversized handle-switch.

Another gunshot *crack* of electricity, but this time she was front and fucking center. She snapped her hands to the top of her head and full-body recoiled, but her eyes couldn't move away from the former cyberfucker.

They twitched and writhed intermittently, each violent wrench of their overtaxed body complete with a new waft of acrid electronic smoke. They gurgled and panted, their subconscious firing on all pre-singed neurons to try to keep the body alive. Despite it all, a twisted, feral smile, accented by froth and drool, was dug into their face. They were dead, but alive.

Kyle felt her stomach turn over and fought to keep Violet and her long-digested breakfast down.

An older domme put her hand on Kyle's shoulder, a leather angel in her serenity, in the Mona Lisa half-smile that drags you in and raises your hackles in unknowing terror. Her voice was a low tenor.

"You busy, wolf?"

Kyle blinked slowly, then shook her head.

"I'll give you a hundred dollars if you drag this dead guy to the Recomb."

Hey, that's rent money.

"You got it," Kyle wheezed, and immediately rolled up her sleeves.

Someone somewhere else shouted to kill the power, and she reached for the cords.

6

Afterglow

1:19 p.m.

"Beautiful day."

Kyle let out an exasperated sigh and stood from her slouch to look at the random passerby who had casually asked her attention with those two words. Long hair, long robes, layered up and up and up all over their body in a concentric, stylish mass. Kyle then looked up at the sky, and found the sun's visually dispersed blessing disappearing behind gray and black clouds with roiling undersides meaner than her teeth.

"Looks like it's gonna fucking rain," Kyle rattled out, her lungs still sore from exertion.

"I like rain," the passerby returned simply, a soft smile on their round face.

"Well, we sure as hell get enough rain here."

"We get *monsoons*," they gently corrected, "and usually not at this time of the year."

Kyle let her shoulders relax and looked away from the passerby. They were right, of course. It was usually bone dry this time of year, and even when it rained like usual in the fall and winter, it was always a sideways downpour.

"Yeah," wolf-girl muttered, gazing up in tandem with this random person off the street.

"A relatively gentle rain. It's good for cleansing the soul as much as it is for running some of the dirt off the streets."

"Guess the street sweepers can't get it all."

The clouds came together, little swirls of cloud that must've been miles long brushing into one another like the foamy run-off from a drain pipe.

"Well. Take care now, friend. Enjoy your time with that body."

Kyle blinked rapidly and squeezed her hand, still holding onto her assigned half-corpse's wrist. There was a streak of dark red blood and a few crunched-up bits of plastic in a long trail along the pavement from where she'd dropped them from her shoulder and started dragging them behind her. It looked awfully like a bunch of other faded streaks and circles in the pavement in front of the second clinic.

"Thanks, stranger," wolf-girl returned, shifting her weight awkwardly.

The passerby waved politely with one arm at chest-level, dipped their head, and walked right past Kyle, stepping over her comatose charge in the process.

What a fucking weirdo.

Kyle lifted her right hand to take a cigarette that wasn't there out of her mouth, and then played that off coolly by reaching up to scratch her hair next to her ear. Nobody was paying attention to her anyway - all eyes on the halfway busy sidewalk and street were owned by medical professionals on their mandated breaks, all glazed over with disinterest and fatigue.

In the background, the continuous murmur of thousands of people coming and going from The Circus (and the continuous wails from its sister, Hell) provided an aural backdrop to the fading, muffled dings of overused hospital announcement services and screechy multilingual notices carried by the weak breeze.

Kyle turned back to the front door of the chipped-paint clinic with an A-sign out front that read "Leave your bodies here," with a cute little infographic depicting various degrees of death and destruction wrought on citizens' bodies. 'Self-Triage,' they started calling it, as if someone who's covered in nut and missing their head can determine which entrance they should get wheeled through.

She braced her arm and got back to work.

Kyle dragged the cyberfucker into the clinic foyer, already crowded with bodies, most left in a heap on the floor. It looked less like a medical clinic and more like a morgue crossed with a butcher shop. It smelled a little bit worse than both.

"Hello, may we help you?"

The attendant at the counter waved at Kyle to follow their words. Bits of blood were stuck to their familiar vest, long soaked into the fabric.

"Oh, uh, just bringing this guy in for you."

She motioned to the almost-corpse halfway out the door at her feet.

"Right."

The Kadet here was a bit more jaded - she could tell by the blasé reaction to the froth-mouth cum-pants and continuing nonreaction to the mountain of whimpering gore just a step away. They continued;

"Name, gender, pronouns? For the records."

Oh, fuck off.

Kyle winced and waved her free hand dismissively. She began to talk as she walked, pulling the day's latest victim in behind her.

"Don't worry about the formalities, bud. I'm just dropping off the delivery."

"Leave 'em in the pile, then."

Suckers picked the wrong place to fuck if they hate timeskips.

Kyle awkwardly spread her legs and leaned far forward to use her considerable leverage instead of getting her shoes sticky with half-tried blood that pooled at the mound of the dead and dying. It was simple enough to get this not-quite-a-corpse to their home for the next hour, day, week, or however long it took to reconstitute a body for them.

"Busy day?" Kyle asked, standing up straight.

"Quiet day, actually," the attendant replied.

"Maybe I'll give you my name and shit anyway, then."

A grimace formed from the attendant's resting bitch face.

"What can we help you with?" they asked, deliberate punctuation on every major syllable to try to scare Kyle off.

"I need my stomach pumped," she returned, her pronunciation growing exaggeratedly harsh in response, "because there's a *woman* in there."

A firm exhale through their nose preceded them pounding on their desk keyboard.

"Yeah. I can get you in. About fifteen minutes."

A few more clicks and clacks. Resonant impacts in the eerie, focused quiet of medical bureaucracy.

"Name, pronouns."

Kyle closed her eyes. The voice that came wasn't hers, necessarily. A professional, distanced affect to keep herself level as she lied.

"Kyle Tymoteusz Orlanski. She/her."

Click clack clack.

"Hm. I don't have anything in here. Recent immigrant?"

Deep breath.

Deep breath. In and out, fast enough to not seem weird.

"No, that's just not my legal name. I've been using it for ten years, though."

Clack click clack.

They're going to ask for my name, my real name. If I give it, their eyes are gonna go wide. They'll ask for a fucking autograph. If they ask, I have to walk out.

Kyle's heart rate spiked, mostly felt in her throat and her ears. A few moments later, behind her eyes, still sealed shut.

"Okay, Kyle T. Orlanski. That's fine. It's an in-and-out on a slow day, just take a seat."

Are there any not occupied by meat?

"Thank you."

The disassociated divide between her thoughts and her actions carried over to her lazily striding to the back wall, farthest from the bodies, until the moment her rear touched the assumedly disgusting seat.

Just relax.

Kyle bobbed her left foot, hand on her knee.

Don't think about Violet.

She was thinking about Violet, of course, because of the mound of disfigured corpses in the corner. While Kyle hadn't been party to any of their spectacularly grisly and intensely sensual deaths, some of them passed as acid-bath analogues in her grim, anxious mind.

She bit back a little hot bile in the back of her throat. Heartburn or worse.

Don't fucking think about it.

The minutes passed, the slow-roll pulse of nausea in waves forcing her to hyperventilate and focus on not thinking to keep her breakfast and whatever was left of her lover down. Sure, they'd still take care of her if she was left in a puddle on the ground, but this was expeditious. A delivery to get her back to work, back to life, faster.

A comically cruel tick-tick-ticking of an ancient, analogue wall-clock above Kyle's head thundered more loudly in her tall ears the more close to a full panic attack she was.

A few times, Kyle thought her claws went through her denim. Never quite, but the tips still hurt enough to distract. She squeezed harder the faster she breathed. Right at the blurred edge between breakdown and conscious pain, she thought her cuticles might be bleeding.

"Uh, Kyle Orlanski?"

"Yes! Yes, here," she shouted, her voice relieved and fragile.

A doctor held open a door to her right, mercifully away from the pile of gore for someone else to deal with. They immediately ducked back into the hallway, a blur of white and red that had a hundred things better to do.

"Come with me. Stomach pump."

Kyle nearly leapt up. She snapped her sore left hand from her knee to her chest, just above her stomach, as if a mild pressure from outside could cork the bottle of her angry indigestion. She spoke as swiftly as she imagined the operation going;

"Let's make this quick, I'm sure you've got a lot to do today."

The doctor spoke, but didn't turn, as they led her on.

"You said there's another person in your stomach, yes?"

"Yeah, that's why-"

"How long have they been in there?"

Kyle reached her right hand across her waist and pulled out her phone to check the time.

"Uh - hour and a half? Two? Something like that."

The doctor about faced and stopped, their blood-spackled lapel half-gleaming from the brilliant glow of the UV lights lining the ceiling. Sophia Acker, she/her. Between the thick crow's feet in the corners of her narrow eyes and the uncovered, tight bun on the back of her head, she looked like the single most average motherfucker this city had to offer. Even her eyes were a completely normal brown.

"Change of plans. I numb you, give you an incision, go in that way."

Kyle towered over her, but the way Dr. Acker's eyes unerringly bored into hers, she felt like she was looking up.

"What kinda cut?" she managed to squeak out.

"I'll see when I get there. Subcostal or Bevan, probably."

"I'm-"

Not exactly medically literate?

"If you want, you can watch."

Kyle's voice quaked.

"I'd really hate that, doc."

"Mhm. Take this."

The doctor thrust a clipboard that had always been there but that Kyle had never noticed right into the latter's waiting right hand. There was a pen attached by a small plastic chain that jingled loose and free, no longer held in place with the doctor's professional grip.

"Read and sign when we get to the room, and we'll get you and your friend sorted."

The doctor turned and motioned with a hand to continue following.

She's a lot better than a friend.

"She's not my friend."

Kyle winced, but followed.

She found herself in a room much like one that morning, albeit a little more packed-in with gear and substantially warmer. Middle of the day, and obviously regularly in use - the light stains on the walls and tile did a lot to add to the menacing qualities of familiar long boxes hanging up, waiting for their time to hungrily stab and suture limbs.

Like this morning.

All at once, the length of time Kyle'd been awake hit her like a truck. A gentle fugue to detach her ego from her senses, and from the awareness of burning heat under her skin, and old, greasy sweat in her fur; she only came to from the toolbox jingle of a dozen scalpels. The multi-tool pop of cheap, perfectly sanitary plastic and metal. She turned to find the doctor setting up an uncharacteristically clean tray with bright and shiny blades and a couple retractors. Big ones.

"Uhh. I haven't, uh, signed the thing yet, doc."

"You will."

Kyle's voice was as uncertain as the doctor's was determined.

"Right. I'll get on that."

She didn't bother reading all the medical legalese, the release forms and unending small text bullshit. None of it mattered. What fucking liability was held?

Maybe if she stabs my heart I'll get out of paying rent.

Kyle snorted and wrote her fake-signature and the date onto the bottom line of the third page. Kyle T. Orlanski, August 6th, 2132.

Ten years.

Somewhere behind her left eye, the distinct memory-sight of a bus' high-beams blocked out her real vision for a second.

She almost didn't hear the doctor calling her name.

"Orlanski?"

Kyle blinked four or five times, painfully. Her eyes were sore from lack of rest, and it felt like little needles lined the lids.

The doctor had wheeled her cart over to the side of the chair in the middle of the room, and aligned a few large, distinct, and undefinable device-boxes around where she would presumably stand. Above Kyle's non-existent pay grade, of course.

"You can sit here if you've signed," the doc continued.

"Yeah."

"Please take off your jacket and shirt, though."

Kyle pulled denim and polyester over her head, and left both by the door. She strode up to the chair and extended the clipboard to the doc, who thoughtfully put it somewhere behind her, out of sight, out of mind. She only had eyes for the door, long since closed behind the three of them. Couldn't forget the reason Kyle was here, after all.

She sat down in the chair, vastly too small for her. The back of her head hung over the top of the headrest, and the stiff padding provided no comfort for her long neck. Her knees likewise hung in the air.

Bet I look like a clown.

"I'll need you to hold still. I don't need to use knockout gas for this. Just mind your breathing."

The doctor pulled a set of shifting but tightly-set slats over, and set it onto Kyle's chest. The seconds nearly perfectly conformed both to her form, and to her breathing. They rose and fell with every shallow inhale, blocking sight of everything going on behind it.

"Once you feel this little prick," the professional continued, invisible behind the fence, "you won't feel a thing. Don't talk, breathe shallowly."

Visions of scalpels and hands rooting around in her. Manic or dispassionate eyes behind blood-splattered glasses. Kyle's heart painfully twitched a few extra times between beats.

"I really hate this part, doc."

"Quiet."

Kyle shut up. She felt a needle enter just below her breast, and then a hot wave pulsed out across her body from there. No less anxiety, but at least now her fingers and toes tingled and she very literally felt nothing. Kyle ficked her eyes around the room, soaking in as much stimulus as possible to try to slow down the panic attack beating on the walls of her brain.

The sounds were small and yet horrific. Wet peeling and stretching, sounds of meat and drops of wet on the floor. The noises of her body being shifted around in ways not naturally meant, at the edges of her hearing. Noises that echoed like thunder in her mind, the backing chorus to a rising scream of tension.

Quiet. Please.

"Ah. I'm in and I see your friend. We'll be done in a minute."

Kyle opened her shaking lips to say 'oh, already?' as if it hadn't felt like she'd been sitting down for half a goddamn hour. She let her jaws naturally come together again to prevent the extra work of her lungs from getting in the way.

There was a shake of something translucent and white out of the corner of her eye. Plastic clicking against metal. Kyle felt her whole body pushed to one side, and then connected that to the sudden loud whirr of a vacuum.

Oh.

Several thunks barely vibrated through the sleepy nerves in her body, deep inside and away from the injection and scalpel.

"Almost done."

Fucking please.

Every detail of the ceiling was so crisp in Kyle's wide, dry eyes. Her body flexed under the doctor's grasp as something was going on behind the divider.

Clink clink. Clack. Stretch. The sensation of something heavy pressed against her whole chest. Every tiny click was a screaming man's fist breaking through the crumbling wall of her already flimsy composure.

Kyle tasted blood. She was really squeezing her teeth *hard*.

Her fingers gripped the chair tight. She shrunk as far into the corner of her mind as she could. Her body forced itself to retain the same, shallow breath, second after minute. She hyperventilated a little harder every time the slamming sound of medicine happened outside.

Her body was going to be fine. She stifled a scream that would extend from her mindscape to the real and merge the two when she *really* couldn't handle that.

I so need you to be done, doc.

Strangely calm thoughts inside a screaming mind.

"We're done. Take a deep breath, Orlanski."

Mind and body came together again as Kyle took a deep, deep breath. Nothing was attached to her chest, and the doctor took away the shifting divider to reveal nothing but smooth fur and a line of stitches just under the sag of her breast to match the ones already fading away in her leg.

"That sucked," Kyle hissed, tracing her fingers over what used to be an incision wide enough to hold her whole fucking chest open.

"Imagine how your friend felt," the doctor replied impassively.

Probably fucking liked it you asshole cunt.

"Yeah. Maybe."

Of course she'd imagined it. She'd imagined every lurid detail of her now totally empty stomach had ravaged Violet's beautiful little body, and just thinking about those thoughts had her cock twitching behind unmoving denim jeans.

The doctor extended a hand, with a pair of bright blue pills, perfectly round and completely unstamped.

"Take these two with some food in a few minutes. Antibiotics for today. They'll probably make you a little sick, so be careful."

Wolf-girl extended her hand and let her medicine fall to it. The second the doctor looked away, she popped them dry into her mouth and swallowed them down.

"Gotcha doc. Can I go?"

"You can go."

God, finally.

She stood, though her whole body still tingled with anesthetics. Dizzy. Unbalanced. She managed to stagger up to the door and grab her tops, throw them on, and then walk back the way she came.

The smell was horrible. Even worse, now that her sense of touch was so dulled as to heighten the other five. There were a few more corpses on the pile, some clothed, some not.

Kyle walked past, trying not to gawk any longer than she had to to step over outstretched and twitching arms.

Outside wasn't much better. Someone was cooking meat, or a substitute, or her brain was misfiring - probably that one - on the corner. The splatter of new, fresh rain rounded out the edges of their hawking cries and the conversations of people milling around, waiting for their order.

But that *smell.*

Kyle's head swam, and she ducked into the alley between the clinic and the next building over. Away from all the smells and sights and *smells.* Her hand found purchase against the slimy brick, and she leaned heavily on it.

She imagined Violet, pristine and beautiful, to try to center herself.

Then the pile of corpses pushed their way into her mind at the same moment the wind beat on her back, carrying the smell of cooking meat.

There was a little tingle of spice on her tongue and in her nose.

That spice rose up her throat, and her eyes snapped open wide in involuntary panic as she held her breath and fell to her knees.

She vomited, a watery heave of nothing but a few trickles of speckled bile and tainted medical saline left over on the pavement. In the middle were those two pills, no longer blue, and significantly smaller just from the few minutes inside her.

Kyle's eyes flickered as she sucked in humid summer-rain air.

Without outside stimulus, her mind's eye filled in the gaps and imagined those pills as Violet. Her body singed by acid and all her soft tissues worn away.

Why had there been more than one thunk on the vacuum?

Her eyes snapped open as she groaned, trying desperately not to think. Right on those two pills. Right into the multicolored bile at her knees.

How much of this is her?

She heaved again.

She started crying from the pain.

She heaved again.

Nothing else came up but her tears.

7

Dicknapped
2:00? 2:30? 3:00? p.m.

Kyle managed to get herself back together on the other side of a dumpster in the alleyway, where it shielded her from the smell of her own vomit. There was no nausea left in her after such a retching, but it was best to distance herself from any reminder of the last few minutes. Or fifteen minutes. Or half an hour.

The sun was still hidden by the roof of black clouds. Any sense of the passing time would have to wait until wolf-girl looked at her phone, but all she wanted to look at was the opposite wall of the alley, at the bricks picking up condensation and stray flecks of rain.

She was so tired. Tired from her ears to her feet. Tired in her hands and her chest. Tired down to the core of her sore body, deprived of food and anesthetics. Tired to the very core of her mind and its free-wheeling gears of thought. One of those gears thought maybe it'd be a good idea to lay down in the garbage and take a long, long nap. Something to make up for the night of sleep she'd missed out on a day ago.

She managed to sniffle a few times. She was too tired to cry anymore.

Kyle thought about closing her eyes, but only managed to keep blinking.

The sound of footsteps, loud and clear, rang down the alleyway.

Defying exhaustion through no will of her own, wolf-girl stood and clenched her fists and turned to face whoever approached. Their voice carried before they came fully into view;

"Hey, are you okay?"

Deep, but with a feminine affect. Some intangible lilt of syllables that intuitively made sense in Kyle's weary brain.

"No."

A very matter-of-fact response from Kyle, her lips and fists trembling in equal measure.

The light caught the approaching person; they were short, maybe only coming up to Kyle's chest, skinny, wore a sweater vest over long sleeves, chinos, and probably real leather shoes. Most notably, though, was the four arms, and shoulder-length hair that covered one or both of their eyes, depending on which way they held their head.

"Could I maybe help you, then?"

Kyle's arms started to shake, too.

"No, fucking get away from me."

Desperately, she reached for anything to tack on.

"Only freaks hang out at the backs of alleys."

Their face scrunched from the top. Their bangs made it impossible to tell if they were furrowing their brows, but that was Kyle's safest assumption.

"You're also at the back of the alley, dude."

Kyle spat out her response before it even attempted approval in her head.

"Yeah, and I've got a whole fucking load of hateful shit to say about myself."

The visitor took another step closer, placing their lower arms' palms together.

"Is this why you're sitting in trash and crying?"

"Eat my whole ass, cunt. Suck my cock and choke."

They smirked. Their teeth looked pretty. A glimpse at really immaculate dentistry.

I want to break them.

"Look, clearly we got off on the wrong foot..."

Oh, I got a good one for you, bud.

"I'll shove my foot in your mouth."

They inhaled sharply, and exhaled slowly.

"Why don't we start over? My name is Inanna. What's yours?"

Kyle's lips couldn't stop twitching. She nearly didn't manage to get the sounds out right.

"Kyle, she and her."

"And they and them for me."

Silence between them, the sound of pattering rain on awnings high above.

"You sound like you're having a very, very bad day today," they continued. They took another step closer.

"Maybe I could be a friend for you, for at least a few minutes. Would you like that?"

Kyle snorted. She crossed her arms, some of her nerves having dissipated in the huff.

"What're you gonna do, ask to borrow some money? I don't have any."

"Have you, maybe, considered that you're alone because of this attitude?"

Yeah, I have, and yeah, you're right.

"Fuck you."

"All I'm saying," Inanna groaned, "is to try to let someone in who wants to help, right?"

Kyle stamped her foot, a pitiful squish of boot into wet paper mash.

"What, do you want my fucking life story? Why I ended up the sexiest piece of shit crying in an alleyway next to her sick?"

Inanna's voice was quiet.

"Well, actually, that is what I'm asking."

Kyle stamped again, rolled her eyes, and dug her fingers into the denim around her forearms.

"Fine. I'm a trans woman who ran away from home in my teens, stole a bunch of money, and got furry surgery so I wouldn't look like my famous shithead parents any more.

"I'm out here because I couldn't sleep, got called at three or four in the fucking morning, and got roped into a wild goose chase to find some guy I fucked's home, which probably doesn't actually exist, turns out!

"I was vomiting because I ate one of the only people who showed me real, personal kindness for days. I got nauseous thinking about it."

A pause, before she continued to cut off their question.

"Yes, it was a sex thing."

"It always is," they responded with as much politeness as they could manage.

"I'm not getting into more details unless you buy me beer, weed, a meal, or all three."

Inanna gripped their bottom two hands together, the top two resting on their hips.

"Were you being facetious about the   dick comment earlier?"

Wolf-girl snorted and shook her head incredulously.

"I'm not gonna fuck you. I already jerked it and had my emotional breakdown about it today. I'm not looking for another."

They didn't skip a beat.

"Would you like some advice?"

"Oh my god, sure, why the fuck not, right? Maybe you'll leave me alone afterwards."

Inanna took another step closer. Kyle didn't budge. She imagined they took that as encouragement, and strode right up to the towering coyote's side, there between the dumpsters.

"May I touch you?"

Kyle grimaced.

"No."

Probably for your own sake from all this fucking filth.

"That's okay. I think you should know that, despite everything, people love you. People *will* love you, even if no-one does right now."

"Great speech, Ina."

"Well, I'm not done!"

Kyle rolled her eyes and rolled her wrist, motioning for them to continue.

"Things are weird and uncertain, and journeys are hard! But you shouldn't feel like you've messed up just because a bunch of things didn't go your way. You've learned, you've developed relationships, you've gained new memories. Even bad memories are important - for everyone! Tomorrow will be better, statistically - and even if it isn't, the next will be. Every day of suffering is a building block to a better personal future, as long as you keep going."

Wolf-girl blinked slowly. She felt her expression relax every moment that they spoke to her, that particular, unflappable lilt of positivity pulling down the walls around her heart. When Kyle finally spoke again, her voice crackled.

"I'll, uh. Keep that in mind."

"You're welcome. I hope you think about this all day, no matter what happens."

Kinda weird, but alright.

They continued;

"Is that your bike?"

Inanna pointed with their top left arm, bottom left below it with an open palm. Two gestures for the price of one, both at the scuffed-up behemoth that Kyle had parked just across the street.

"Yeah, that's my bike. Do you like bikes?"

"A little. I know how to ride one."

Kyle couldn't help but smile.

"Yeah, you know, maybe you're alright," Kyle grumbled, a note of quiet acceptance beneath the gravel.

"Sadly, I have to go **now**-"

Their words ended in exertion. Kyle felt a rush of wind -

Flash of light. Ringing ears. Blitzing pain in her head. Numb-pain at the base of her skull, agony radiating to the front, right above her eyes. Trauma-sensations sent her brain into an over-stimulus fugue. Impossible to move, to feel, to anything, to - *God that fucking ringing would you STOP you're worse than an alarm clock -*

wait.

Kyle experimentally teased her eyes open, wary of light, to find nothing at all except an LED readout, faded red behind aged plastic. Her head throbbed with each harsh screech of the alarm coming from that light. All else she could tell in the dark was that this was not the alleyway she was just in.

She forced her pain-blurry eyes to focus on the clock.

6:51 pm.

Oh fuck.

Wolf-girl quickly assessed her limbs, and while she couldn't see them, or, for some reason, feel them, she imagined the thought-feeling associated with moving them and figured that was enough to rise.

The alarm quit of its own accord just a second after she sat up, some kind of motion sensor in the dark. Suddenly bereft of an artificial headache, Kyle could hear something much more concerning. Whatever she was sitting on was crunchy, and densely so.

She clenched her fists, felt the nails dig into her palms. A cold numb.

She started to sweat, despite shivering.

Kyle frantically clapped her hands together and rubbed for her life, forcing warmth back into her most bloodless extremities. They started to *sear* as they rose up to body temp again. She stopped just to reach one cold-burned hand down to her seat.

Crunchy, slowly melting ice that burned her confused nerves.

Fucking what did they take?!

Kyle slapped widely around her, looking for the edges of what she assumed was a tub. Her open palms rung out with the tell-tale hollow thunk of porcelain and steel. She wrapped her stinging fingers around the edge and wrenched her sensationless legs over one side, to half-feel the bottoms of her feet touch something firm. A floor, presumably.

Despite feeling less than nothing from the waist down, Kyle forced herself to stand. Her knees and her hips shook mightily from the effort. Miraculously, she didn't even fall down.

Progress.

Like she'd searched for the edges of the tub, she started searching herself. Open palms and scrabbling fingers, touching all about her chest - still wearing her shirt, but not her jacket - *no incision marks*. She then counted her static-pain fingers - *all ten*. She ran her fingers up her neck, stroked her face - *no new marks*.

These minutes dragged on and more and more life flowed through Kyle's body. She could feel all her toes, and by extension, both her legs, though they still felt like gelatin with needles. She reached for her tail for good measure - *also there*. Kyle felt in the dark for a wall, desperate for a light switch.

Two of her bumbling fingers stubbed themselves on just that, and she recoiled from the wall in pain, and from the light in a different kind of pain, as the room fully illuminated.

Kyle slowly opened her eyes, blinking again and again to let them adjust to the harsh, artificial white now flooding the obvious basement. Just to the side of the tub, spanning the entire wall, was a tool rack, nearly white with a thick layer of undisturbed dust, save for two blue pills on a bright white piece of printer paper. The floor, however, was clean, despite both the natural distortion of age and the giant puddle of tacky blood in the middle. A small envelope lay between the puddle and the bench.

She looked down and noticed she wasn't wearing pants. Just a wrapping of a makeshift gown around her waist.

Huh.

Kyle's thighs seared with new pain as she carefully walked around the puddle and scooped up the envelope. It was unbelievably hard for her to kneel, and then to stand again. Like there was a knife stabbing into her crotch.

Inside was a note, typed out and printed and smelling of fresh ink. Kyle's brow furrowed as she forced her eyes to focus and read.

"Hey, Kyle! It's Inanna! Sorry about all this... I have rent to pay myself, and do you know how much authentic untouched estrogenized penis and testicles sell for on the black market? Like, really! It's incredible!

Anyway, I made the cleanest incisions I could, but I don't have access to a medical-grade stitcher, sooooo I closed you up by hand (always do!) and made you an ice bath and hopefully that plugged up the bleeding for a while! ^_^;

Anyway, I drove you here after knocking you out! You still have your phone and your wallet and your bike's outside! That's what I used to get you here, of course! Just in case it wasn't obvious with your brain all scrambled like it probably is. >_<

Good luck!

- Inanna! xoxo"

Kyle's hands shook, but it was more from the lingering frostburn and the increasing awareness of the waves of pain wracking her body than the anger in her slowly thumping heart.

My mind is crystal, you fucking puke.

She squeezed both of her fists tighter than tight, crumpling and shredding the note between her claws as they dug deep into her palms.

And then, all at once, she sighed.

It's not worth losing more blood.

What little was left of the note fell from Kyle's hands into the puddle at her feet. She dropped both of her hands, and carefully unwrapped the linen around her waist. Just as said and expected, her nethers were bare, and there was nothing but the natural curve of her pelvis, stitches, and blood clotting her fur up her happy trail, and down her thighs.

A little bit of cold, dark blood, thick and syrupy, dripped from the poorly-sealed wound.

I've lost a lot of blood today.

Her heartbeat picked up.

I can't lose any more blood.

Kyle knew that she'd run out of adrenaline soon, and then she'd be at the whims of whatever energy her body could muster up from the bare slivers of fat stored around her body. Whatever dregs of nicotine and caffeine that still puttered around in her half-empty veins.

Plastic bags. Antibiotics.

Wolf-girl knew she had to use what clarity she had while she had it. With her right hand, she scooped up the familiar two pills off the desk and wolfed them down. With her left hand, she opened a drawer, rustled around in it, and then closed it. Then did the same with two new drawers, with both hands. Repeat. After a minute or ten of deliberate searching, she managed to find an old, but sealed, box of plastic bags.

Ice.

She leaned back over the tub, doing her best not to flex her thighs or stretch her abdomen too badly. She shoved in fresher, less-melted ice from well beneath the surface she'd laid on, noting the dribbles of frozen blood webbing between them.

God, I hope I didn't lose too much.

Kyle felt dizzy because she imagined she should really be feeling dizzy.

I lost a lot. Fuck.

The linen gown wasn't very thick, so she grabbed hold of one edge with her teeth and ripped off about two square feet, wrapped the bag of ice in it, and then shoved it into her mutilated groin.

Kyle let out a long, hollow wail of pain as soon as the coarse fabric touched her stitches.

It took her a few minutes to be able to gather up her consciousness again, and then gather up her clothes and belongings scattered around the room. Kyle grit her teeth and choked down a sob-scream as she clenched the bag in her weak thighs to free both her hands to get her jacket back on.

This isn't the worst thing that's ever happened to me.

It wasn't entirely a lie, but the brain fog crept in enough to keep her wildly cruel imagination from conjuring up any of those memories. The impact of such was enough to get her to finally realize the trouble she was in.

I lost a lot of blood.

She'd lost a lot of blood.

There was a backpack in the corner that Kyle shoved her pants and phone and anything else she believed was hers in, and slung it over her back. She pushed her shoes on and didn't tie them up. Every single movement was a tactical, deliberate expenditure of what little energy she had, the smallest necessary, the fewest necessary.

The door to the outside opened easily, as if this decrepit basement were brand new. She blinked and somehow had gone up half a flight of steps, her arm holding the backpack quivering at her side.

Put it on your back, idiot.

Kyle slung it over her right shoulder, keeping the ice between her legs in place with her left arm. She very consciously walked up the rest of the steps, small, pathetic screams dying in her sore throat.

The door at the top opened just as easily, and right next to her was her bike.

Fuck you. Fuck you, cunt.

Wolf-girl spat on the ground at the bottom of the front wheel.

She sidled up to the seat and managed to plant her ass side-saddle. Left arm still occupied, she reached under her left knee with her right hand, and with an unrestrained scream of pain, lurched it over the other side.

She felt fresh, hot blood dribble against all her fingers.

Fuck.

Kyle took a second to lean her forehead against the dash, scream again until she ran out of breath, then lean back to a regular riding pose. It was hard to see the end of the alley, half from her fading clarity, and half from welling tears of pain.

Fuck.

She tore a few more stitches kicking up the kickstand, and then she revved down the alleyway and onto the road, into the dense evening traffic.

8

Like a man wandering the desert, drunk on the sun
Sometime after 7:00 p.m.

Kyle rolled her bike to a stop at a useless red light with zero cross-traffic. For just a moment, her one-handed grip on the handles faltered, and so followed the brakes. The front wheel skidded through a tiny puddle, and the seat bucked up. Unbelievable pain, like a fist pushing through her. She grit her teeth and seethed out a long whine, and pressed the wet ball of cold linen harder against her groin.

Fresh red blood trickled past the malformed clots woven in between inadequate stitches.

God fucking dammit.

Wolf-girl managed to flutter her eyes open to look around her. One car behind her. None crossing the intersection. Normally she'd sigh, kick the ground, rev the motor, light a cigarette, or any other of a dozen frustrated little rituals to vent a little annoyance into the world.

Instead, she did nothing. Kyle let her body relax as much as she dared, for fear of passing out in the seat and simply dying on the street. Nobody was gonna give a fuck about the third near-corpse they'd seen that day. Not the driver behind her, busy getting somewhere they need. Not the pedestrians, currently absent due to the still-spitting rain. Certainly not the cop waiting at the stoplight for the crosswalk to turn white.

Wait.

A cop on foot?

Wait.

Kyle heard an audible crunch of realization in her head. She summoned all the resolve in her throat and all the breath in her lungs to shout;

"HEY, PIG!"

They turned immediately. Skin so pale it reflected the light off the fading sun into her eyes. Uniform so black and red nobody would ever notice the bloodstains in the fabric.

God fucking help me.

"DO YOU KNOW WHERE THE NEAREST CLINIC IS?"

They tilted their head to one side, and slightly away. Kyle must've looked almost unique; a seven foot tall furry bleeding out on a motorbike that *absolutely* wasn't street legal, calling them the only slur they ever cared about.

Their voice returned, distant despite how close they were. Kyle's senses were absolutely dulled beyond proper use. Their voice was the most stereotypical Canadian drawl you could imagine, all the vowels rounded out, the consonants short and deemphasized.

"Uh, yeah, if you go down about four blocks and hook a right, you should be there lickity split, bud."

"Thanks, bacon," Kyle gasped out.

They opened their mouth to say something, but the light turned green. The tone of the crosswalk beeped loud. The cop turned away and settled for;

"No... no problem, bud. You stay safe now."

Kyle nodded. They waved slightly. Green light and white light, they both crossed the same road, together, apart. She didn't let her shoulders unclench until she couldn't feel their eyes on her back any longer.

Dodged a fucking bullet.

A tiny, wry smile as that spurt of overused adrenaline petered out.

Maybe literally.

Kyle dared a tiny sigh.

Probably.

The light stayed green for the next street, and she rolled through the intersection as smoothly as she could manage. Her head lolled to one side on a small bump, and there she let her eyes rest for just a second,

and opened them two streets away, stopped at a red light.
Ah, uh-
She tried to blink herself awake, to awareness,

but only caught herself again when she rolled over a curb and nearly hit a pedestrian in a bright yellow raincoat. Kyle inhaled *hard* through her nose-

"JESUS FUCK-"

And managed to wobble out of their way, barely avoiding both a crash and a suicide-murder. The front and back wheels dipped and rattled her *hard* as she dropped back onto the street. Kyle's whole body throbbed in hot, radiating pain. The proverbial knife between her legs twisted.

A little hot bile splashed against the back of her throat, but there was simply no energy left to retch.

This was the corner the pig had said to turn at, and sure enough, a sign to Kyle's right confirmed as much. Five hundred meters. Every time she blinked, she again jolted forward through space and time.

Why am I doing this?

Kyle clutched the bag tighter to her, again. Her hand was shaking, and it was hard to keep a grip with the blood between her knuckles.

I want to die so badly. Always have.

The sickly crimson sign of a clinic reflected on the rainy ground in front of her. She drove over the curb and parked sideways in two of the open spots.

I don't get why I don't let myself go.

She remembered to put the kickstand down, as much as it hurt to flex her mutilated pelvic floor.

I really hope I pass out before I reach the door.

Kyle passed through the front door, leaving a bloody, furry handprint on the glass.

Well, whatever. Answers are for smart people.

Kyle staggered in, walked straight past the waiting area, and slammed her free fist on the counter.

"I invoke the Emergency Abuse Act," she wheezed.

The receptionist's name was Abigail, she/her, according to her shiny lapel, and she/her stood as quickly as her eyebrows hit her scalp.

The Emergency Abuse Act was a bill rammed through the federal government as soon as being transgender became vogue for mainstream politicians, and as soon as it became 'woke' for people to just fuck around with their bodies. It was a bill designed to fast-track gender reassignment surgery and help kids with shitty parents get to safety; this receptionist probably had never fucking heard of it, since it was superseded by a million-and-one bills since, but the name was deeply alarming and it got Kyle in before she bled to death.

She *really* didn't want to have any memory lack. She *really* didn't want to deal with the philosophical implications of her first death.

"That means," *breath*, "you get," *breath*, "a surgeon," Kyle explained. She could barely keep her eyes up. Gravity dragged her vision to the sticky blood on the hand she leaned against the receptionist's desk with.

"I'll get a surgeon."

Such fucking determination. Maybe there's still a soul left in the medical business.

Kyle blinked again, and opened her eyes to her head slumped against the glass divider, and the sensation of four hands pressed against her shoulders.

"Get the *fuck-*" she started, eyes snapping open wide with a jolt. Kyle's adrenal gland had been wrung dry, though, and a split second of energy to flip around was all she got before it screamed for rest and slammed the door on her heart again. The sound of the back of her head hitting the plexiglass was hollow.

Kyle felt hollow.

There were four medical professionals, wearing scrubs and aprons and surgical masks. They were fucking ready for her. The tallest spoke first, voice deep but muffled, their lips shifting inscrutably while hidden behind the classic triple-layered polypropylene.

"You've lost a lot of blood."

Oh my god. No shit.

"We have a room for you. Please let us help carry you there."

Two nurse-looking types stepped forward, their hands tentatively outstretched. They weren't going to do shit without Kyle's consent. She roll-nodded-dropped her head, a begrudging and exhausted sigh whistling between her teeth.

Four strong hands that helped her away from the counter, and that helped support her as she walked. Blood, new and old, dripped down her legs and freely from her loins to mark her passage. Despite everything, all she could smell was sanitizer, and all she could hear was the paper rustle of disposable clothes. Only one statement came to mind.

"I *hate* this part, doc."

The first doctor turned while walking, and returned, bemused;

"I bet you say that every time you go to one."

Kyle grimaced, but couldn't muster up the energy to feign being mad any more.

Got me there, labcoat.

"You don't have to sign right now," another said, waving a clipboard with one hand, "but we'll need some basic information. What genitals are you looking to get?"

Kyle's eyelids twitched, as if she could close them and wake up fine, somewhere else. She knew, though, she *had* to follow through.

Dick, balls. Make the bigger decision later.

"Vagina."

Oh. Cool.

Her mouth trembled like she was crying. The paperwork doctor continued;

"Roger. If you pass out now, we know what to do. Can we get a name for the record?"

Instead of her heartbeat quickening, her throat nearly closed up.

Say Kyle Tymoteusz Orlanski.

She hesitated, mouth open.

Say Kyle Tymoteusz Orlanski.

Her quivering lips disobeyed.

"Christophe de Leon-Lance."

You goddamn fool. WHY.

The doctors and nurses stopped simultaneously. Kyle nearly fell to the floor from her momentum. One leaned forward and put their masked face into view of her slumped head.

"Are you... perhaps related-"

"Yes. Please don't talk about it."

"Yes, ma'am."

Fuck you.

Kyle summoned enough strength to grab this one doctor by the scruff of their scrubs, and pulled them face-to-face. Her voice rattled with fury.

"I'm nobody. Kyle. Kyle T. Orlanski. I'm not - I'm not *his*."

The doctor with the clipboard scribbled quickly.

"Kyle T. Orlanski," they affirmed.

"Goddamn right," Kyle choked out.

The staff helped her through a door, and then collectively scooped her up and laid her out on an actual operating table. High fucking honor, given the shitty chairs she'd been stitched up in repeatedly the for the past twenty four fucking hours. As soon as Kyle thought she might let her eyes flutter closed, paper and pencil were shoved into her blood-matted hands.

"I know it's a hassle, but please sign."

Kyle managed the strength to draw a straight line somewhere near the bottom of the paper. She put a dot near a third through, as if that'd be enough for the T. The nurses and doctors' voices all mingled as they began final preparations.

At some point she blinked and her jacket and shirt were gone.

Makes sense.

Someone shoved a needle into her right arm and set up a bright red bag on an IV pole.

Barely... hurt.

"Do you wanna be knocked out, or awake?" someone asked.

What the fuck... kinda question is... that?

Even her inner monologue was gasping for breath.

"Put me the fuck under," she spat out in one shallow breath.

"Alright."

The inquirer turned and fiddled with hard, heavy plastic out of view. Rattling clunks and rustling bits of medical horror at their fingertips, for her pleasure.

"Count your heartbeats for me," they continued.

With her hands free of paperwork and ice, she counted. One beat. Left index. Two beat. Right index. Three beat. Left middle. Four beat. Right middle. Slow and steady, but heavy. Terror coursing in the place of adrenaline.

The attendant wheeled back around, and two more professionals briskly entered the room, tying back their aprons. The syringe in one's hand looked more like a turkey baster in its hideous girth. Kyle stared at it, but kept counting. Her fingers shook harder as she extended them in time with her quickening heartbeat.

"Who taught you to count like that?"

"Wha- huh?"

She put her palms flat on her legs, a little dry blood on her palms getting refreshed from her still-oozing nothing.

"Alternating hands. That's novel," they continued.

"We... I didn't really... didn't really count much... growing up, I guess?"

"Could you turn your left arm to me?"

She did so, palm up. He poked the tip of that monstrosity against her arm, adjusted its seating, adjusted his seating, and then looked at her face.

"This is going to hurt a lot for a second. Just bear with it. Take a deep breath. Keep counting the beats."

They slid the needle through her fur, under her skin. It visibly bulged. It hurt like shit, they were right, but like how far distant thunder is loud. She clenched her opposite fist and both of her feet and every other muscle big and small that she could control that was not her left arm, little tears forming in the corners of her narrow eyes, and listened to her heart.

One beat. The pain stopped almost immediately, a warmth spreading all around her. She relaxed her full-body tension.

Two beat. She felt so heavy. So fucking heavy. In an instant she couldn't move, and she was glad she'd unclenched.

Three beat. Her eyes fluttered, a few dark figures strode up to her, and their silhouettes rose high enough to block out the glaring overhead light.

Four beat.

Kyle opened her eyes and was somewhere else.

She tried to say "Oh," but her throat was so dry and so scratchy that it sounded more like the sound of gravel under someone's sneakers.

Am I still bleeding?

With monumental effort, wolf-girl flexed her neck and looked down at her body. She wore a hospital gown that crimped under her armpits, that rode up all the way to her waist. Clearly they'd gotten a kid's size for her.

She woke right the fuck up the moment she saw her groin. It wasn't shaped right.

Oh.

She leaned up a little farther and saw a clear slit dividing two soft mounds under her black crotch fur.

Kyle launched herself feet-first off the recovery bed. That impact felt so different in her core and thighs with her new muscles, her new cavities-

SHUT UP.

She started looking around the room. It was white, sterile, and perfect. The most genuinely professionally medical room in the entire fucking province by her experience.

Where are my clothes?

The sound of clicking shoes on linoleum down the hall. Kyle turned to face the door, consciously working to avoid looking at the gynecology diagrams tacked to it. It swung open, and some nurse-looking type - it was Abigail, still she/her, by the lapel.

Abigail paused in the doorway and stared up at Kyle. Kyle didn't blink, either.

"Uhm," Abigail started.

"Please don't look at my dick."

You don't have a dick anymore.

"My, uh, vag."

Abigail inhaled deeply and let out a long, relaxed sigh.

"Kyle? I was just here to check up on you and get you whatever you needed."

"My clothes, now."

Wolf-girl quivered her lips.

"Sorry. Please."

Abigail motioned with one arm, a silent request to enter. Kyle took a step back to give her the space. The only sound between them was Abigail's shoes clicking on the floor, then the gentle creak of a cabinet, and then the rustle of a backpack full of clothes that she hefted down to the counter for the coyote.

"Sorry," Kyle continued, "thank you."

"I also have a few brochures to help you take care of your new bits, as well as resources to call the police,-"

That'll never happen.

"-so we might be able to catch the person who hurt you."

Kyle nodded. The rustle of her fur under the gown was reassuring. Like it was so quiet here, in this room, so safe, in this room, that the smallest things could be heard. Felt. Appreciated. Abigail cut the silence with her voice again, but it was only slightly jarring.

"If you turn around, you can see your new parts.-"

NO.

"-The mirror is slanted to give you a better look underneath."

Kyle made a mental note to keep that quarter of the room out of her sight.

"You're free to leave as soon as you're dressed. Just go ahead and leave the gown on the bed you woke up on."

Kyle nodded nearly silently. Rustle rustle.

Abigail reached into her pocket and pulled out several folded-up, laminated pieces of paper. Formerly bright colors that had faded from age. One had a funny-looking pink cartoon nubbin on the front - *Clitty, here to tell you how to stay clean and healthy.*

Wolf-girl couldn't look away.

"Hey, Abigail, how long am I -"

She choked on the words for a second.

Hi, Clitty.

Kyle was always a sucker for cartoon mascots.

"How long am I allowed to stay here?"

"As long as you need, Kyle."

Cool, cool.

Kyle's voice was quiet. Her throat shook nearly as much as her lips.

"I'm going to have a complete breakdown in here for a hot minute while I get dressed. I'll leave as soon as I can."

"Take your time. May I touch your arm?"

Kyle wanted to freeze, to shriek, to throw her arm and do her best werewolf impression. Tear Abigail's head clean from her shoulders, ruin all her clothes and this pristine perfect fucking little room. May I *fucking* touch you? Like *Inanna?*

That's a lie. She didn't want that. That was an echo of an echo of a thought, a pathetic squirt of an inkling that didn't even form an emotive sensation in her heart.

"Yeah."

Abigail reached up, and placed one warm, tender palm against Kyle's clean fur.

Kyle collapsed to her knees and clutched Abigail, barely over half her height, tightly.

They held each other for a while, and Kyle apologized the entire time.

-9-

Escapes

It's dark out. Who cares?

The corner McDonalds looked nothing like it had that morning. Instead of just one more too-clean brown and red storefront, appallingly matte in the sunlight, it now glowed with a unique and artificial life well past usual business hours. What else could match the incandescence of surviving Capital, this lifeblood of bleary-eyed drunks, stoners, and people just waking up for their lonely night shifts?

Kyle leaned against the wall outside, not yet willing to join the thin, somber throng inside. She had some nerve to build up. Some gumption. Some wherewithal to push away from the still-damp bricks and repeat her morning performance so she could get some fucking food in her. It was hard to find the will on 48 hours of no sleep, save for a few from anesthesia and head trauma.

Her phone buzzed twice in her pocket.

I'll check it after I get some food.

Kyle twirled an unlit cigarette, over and under her right hand's middle finger. She hadn't smoked since around noon, but whatever residual chemicals in her own and someone else's donated blood kept the craving at bay. Or, maybe, she was just too tired. Too tired to smoke, too tired to steal, too tired to do much else but lean against the bricks and stare out at the harsh, fresh light from the restaurant cast across the old, worn-down street.

Maybe I should quit.

She lifted her hand and gingerly poked the unmarred death stick down into her jacket pocket, down against the side of the carton it came from. It was a lot easier than she'd expected to put it away.

Maybe I should quit.

With a gentle sigh, Kyle pushed herself to stand from the wall. With that same small momentum, she let her feet carry her through the push-pull doors, and into the expected clatter of dishes and food.

"ORDER UP! EIGHTEEN NINETY FIVE, NINETY SIX," called the person at the counter as they placed two to-go bags on the greasy fake-marble.

Kyle slowly walked up to the counter, careful not to draw too much attention, despite her obvious height. She glanced over at the peanut gallery of inebriated geeks - not a one of them had even woken up from their happy stupors to grab one of their meals. All the easier for her to step all the way up, take one hand out of her pocket, and grab the nearer bag by the top.

The low murmur of the restaurant's myriad conversations dipped the same moment her fingers crinkled the brown paper sack. Too loudly. Kyle caught one of the workers in the corner of her eye, and in the pit of her stomach, just before she could react.

"Hey! You didn't pay for that."

Stout and short, neck tattoo, they/shee lapel; Terra, apparently. They stared up at Kyle with crossed arms and a narrow glare. Kyle opened her mouth before she could swallow anxiously, and a little drool dripped out of the corner of her lips.

"Terra, I can explain-"

"Are you hungry?"

Kyle lifted her free hand to wipe away some of the spit from her own face and nodded.

"Y-yes, ma'am."

Kyle pointed behind her with that same hand, the first releasing her white-knuckle grip on the bag of food. She continued;

"I'll go, uh, I'll leave-"

"No, no, nobody goes hungry. That's the country's motto. At least those they don't *want* to go hungry."

Wolf-girl tilted her head, a little confused.

"Just show me which order it was," Terra snapped.

Kyle turned the bag around with two fingers. She sweat bullets. Terra's eyes left Kyle's face for the first time in so many minutes, so they could see which order they'd have to remake.

"Eighteen ninety five. Alright. Just get outta here."

"Sorry. Thanks."

Terra snort-laughed, which drew the attention of someone in the back. Their voice was distant, distorted and covered by the clanging of metal and plastic and oil.

"Who're you lambasting now, huh?"

Terra turned around to walk back into the kitchen, not even giving Kyle the dignity of a condescending staredown on her way out. She didn't have the luck to get out without attention, though.

"Hey, uh, is that my order?"

Kyle snapped her eyes to the voice. A waiting stoner, legs up and feet bare as they laid out in one of the corner booths.

"No, no. Uh. They're remaking yours," Kyle half-lied.

"Oh, cool. Nice jacket."

Her lip twitched.

"Thanks. Goodnight."

Kyle nearly sprinted out of the building with the stoner's bag of food. She thought she heard something like 'Goodnight yourself, tall dark and beautiful!' but it was impossible to tell if that was her imagination talking, as it so often did, or genuine words barely caught beyond the crinkle-crunch of paper and the throbbing of her heart in her tall ears.

Fuck fuck fuck. Fuck fuck. Fuck.

Automatically, she reached into her pocket and pulled out her phone. The stoplight was already white, and there was no traffic to be seen. Wolf-girl tucked her shame under her arm and pounded pavement, desperately trying not to fumble her glass and plastic brick with her shaking hands.

The screen lit up. One missed call, from Dad. One new message, from Dad.

Kyle smoothly picked herself up after nearly falling in the street the moment her conscious mind registered the sender. She'd have to buff out the scuff on the toe of her right shoe later. Her brain was silent, save for the sound of rising static, as she jumped into the text message.

"Hey, sport! I tried calling you, but I guess you were asleep or something, or you might've changed phone numbers, or something. Anyway, I got an e-mail from a clinic down in the city, someone said that my kid had showed up for surgery in an

emergency. *If you're reading this, I'm glad you're still kicking. Please send me a message sometime. Mom and I miss you a lot."*

Kyle bit her bottom lip. The weight in her chest rose to rest directly between her heart and her lungs, and started burning up her throat.

No. No no no. Not for you, prick.

She swiped right with her finger, closing the messenger and leaving it on read.

Kyle kept swiping, back and forth, up and down. Idle fidgets with apps she almost never used. Open a text editor, close it. Lock the phone, then unlock it. Constant motion, her thumb a shark to keep her consciousness from sinking to the bottom of the murk of her soul. Down into the pits of memories that would swallow her up.

She and her bike nearly fell over when she ran into it. A comedy of inattention.

Fuck.

Kyle steadied the bike with the hand not holding her phone, and steadied herself with a step back. Everything was fine. Everything was cool. She hooked her fingers under the inlaid handle of the frunk and popped it open, then crumpled up someone else's food and placed it inside. It clicked shut with just as much ease as that morning.

She stood there for a few seconds or a few minutes, just staring at the rough plastic grain in the low light of a distant street lamp.

It used to be so much whiter. Is it the light?

Kyle dragged one fingertip across the surface, its greebled face gripping well against the leather of her fingertip. It left a tiny streak lighter in its wake.

No, it's just ten years.

The thick plastic groaned slightly as she gripped it tight with her whole hand. Kyle inhaled deeply, held it for a count to ten (seconds? minutes?), and then exhaled through her clenched teeth. It was going to be one of Those Nights.

A late-late night bus slowly crept along the streets, its driver leisurely enjoying the low-stress ride through sleepy mixed-use streets. For a second,

the headlights blinded Kyle through the corner of her eye, until it passed her
and chugged up the hill.

*The flash of light from a bus. The driver stopped on the roadside and asked if I
needed help. I was covered in blood and dirt, and I didn't have fur to hide it. I shouted for
him to help me steal a bike. I lied to him that I was in danger. He helped me.*

Kyle's death grip slackened. She tilted her hand and stroked along
the curve she'd squeezed, as if petting it, as if asking it for forgiveness.

*He asked my name. I lied and said Kyle. He asked for more, so I lied and said
T. Orlanski. I searched for T names a few months later.*

Another sigh seethed its way out of her mouth. Kyle tilted her head
back, her body back, and her leg over the seat to mount *her* bike. With *her* food.

That was a hell of a night. Worst rain I've ever seen.

Kyle flicked up the kickstand and revved the engine. The old fogey of
a bike immediately obeyed, with a stallion's kick to boot. Loud, aggressive.
Bearing scars all over, deep in its plastic and metal, scuffed up stickers Kyle
didn't know when she'd be able to replace. She and her bike flew down nearly
empty streets and kicked up sprays of puddled rainwater that soaked no-one
whenever they hit the bottom of a hill.

She barely had time to notice the "Open 24 Hours" sign of an old-
style hotel above her at a corner she had to turn. From the half-second of
recognition, her mind put together the image of old, dirty light bulbs, colored
with chipped paint and buzzing angrily over her head.

*I'd stayed at a hotel that night, soaked and disgusting. I charged my dad's
card. The food was alright. The best steak I'd ever had.*

Kyle had, much later, had an actually good steak. Turns out hotel
workers are in it for the paycheck, not the artistry. Someone who works at a
restaurant puts in care and effort beyond effort, because they provide only one
service, one service constantly in competition with everyone else. Cutthroat
shit. Life-ruining shit.

Someone who works at a hotel does exactly what they need to do and
no more; their checks aren't dependent on reviews. Their paychecks are
dependent on people needing somewhere to crash for the night. Not like they
don't care, they just don't attract the weirdos willing to put their entire lives on
the line for a pittance and 18-hour work days.

Very average steak. Best steak of my life.

Now, you want bad food? The shit Kyle grew up with-

God, I don't want to think about my parents more.

There wasn't much else for her to think about. The roads droned on and on, and the way home from that oft-robbed McDonalds was so burnt into Kyle's head that she could do it asleep. She was half-dreaming now, her imagination roiling with clouds of memory that took shape and dissipated in record time.

Mom would make absolute garbage food and pretend it was backbreaking for her to do it. I hated it. I hated dry turkey and corn with too much butter.

I wanted to tell her how much it sucked. I wanted to tell her how awful she was. I wanted to tell her all her home-grown blue-collar truths were bullshit.

I wanted to tell her I knew better. I wanted to drill home that I knew what she'd given up. Debt for education, and then not even education.

Ran off with a military man after he got kicked out of his own fucking country.

I wanted to make her hate me. I wanted to make her so angry. So angry she'd pin me to the ground under that "worker's" knee and take up her butcher's knife.

I wanted her to scream and hack at my neck with swings that used her whole body.

I wanted to smile up at her as I felt each blow dig deeper into my sensitive, critical flesh.

I wanted the last few moments of oxygen my brain had to keep me conscious hearing and seeing the world fade away.

I would've smiled through the tears.

Instead, I ate my mashed potatoes quietly and later screamed into a pillow.

Kyle noticed she was gripping the handlebars so tightly the front wheel was shaking. She also noticed she hadn't stopped biting her lip. At a red light, she stopped, popped the frunk, and pulled out one of the greasy napkins from the bag to press to her muzzle.

I've got problems.

Her lip wound wasn't too deep. After another two stops, she threw the half-wet paper towel away to get mulched by moisture in some puddle or the sewers or who gives a *shit* about a piece of fucking paper.

Dad always pointed to his certificates when challenged on anything.

See? Still gonna think about 'em.

God, an entire room of the house was worthless. It was all copies of treaties he'd signed and photos of battlefields and him shaking hands over piles of corpses.

Fucking war hero. Fucking senator. Fucking bum.

Tried to throw him a surprise party and he pointed a gun at me. He didn't even see me in those wide, empty eyes.

Kinda wished he'd pull the trigger. Add one more notch to his fucking belt.

So traumatized. So fucking proud of it, too.

Sobbing into a bottle of vodka while he told me all the evil he'd done.

Laughed into a joint while he told me all about all his dead friends.

It was so scary being alone with him.

Always ended with a sigh and a "What can you do?"

I read his little books on Communism, on Anarchism. I wanted to be smarter than him, better than him.

If I called him on anything, he'd raise a hand. Never hit me, though. He tried so damn hard not to remember 'spare the rod.'

It was so scary being known because of him.

Not even my own person.

Go to town and be fucking invisible next to him. Be fucking invisible unless they wanted me to play basketball for their team. Be fucking invisible until they heard my name.

It's not my name anymore.

Kyle grit her teeth, and felt every rumble of the engine as she revved it in defiance. The streets were empty enough it didn't echo.

I'm not his anymore.

She made a gentle mental note to block his number, later.

I'm Kyle.

Kyle felt a little burning nugget of evil glee. It passed as soon as she noticed it.

Kyle felt so hollow. She didn't know if it was more the lack of genuine sleep for two days, or the memories drowning her imagination in the depths of fourteen years of evil. A little knot still gripped at her heart.

She turned a corner and woke up. It was the corner to the neighborhood with her apartment building. It was pitch black without any street lights.

They say it takes a village to raise a child. I wish they meant that literally. People come and go, kids grow up and leave, and there's new kids to remember. They say that 200 is the maximum number of people that can exist in someone's long term memory. It's reserved for people who matter.

I hope that mom and dad meet enough new people to push me out of their minds completely.

Kyle pulled into the broken garage and pulled the fence shut behind her bike. There was no-one on the streets all night. There was nothing to fear.

It's been ten years, after all.

She pulled out her phone and blocked 'Dad,' and deleted all his messages from her message history. It took a few minutes to delete the decade of text messages.

Kyle walked out of the garage, and through the front door of her apartment building, hollow, but clean.

Alone, Together
Too late.

It was dark in the apartment foyer, like most nights. Dim illumination from bulbs in a line that needed replacement badly, and none from a few that needed it more. In this artificial light, the decades of worn-in paths through the carpet were as evident as the stains. A straight line, right to the elevator in the back - though with a small trail to the left. To the landlord's office.

Kyle's shoes quietly scuffed on the carpet, or whatever was left of it, hard and thin as it was. She raised her left hand, wallet in her fingers, and knocked on the doorframe.

"Mx. Gillespie? I have rent," she called, careful to hit a volume somewhere between 'shouting' and 'considerate to those upstairs.'

The thin wood rattled loudly with each blow of her knuckles, but the hollow echoes attracted no-one. Not even the silverfish scurried from the cracks in the walls.

Must be asleep. Whatever.

Kyle took two steps back, paused to wait for a zero-chance delayed response, then shrugged and walked to the elevator. The wait for it to arrive and the trip up to her floor gave Kyle a good several minutes to think again, much to her continuing chagrin.

Tomorrow morning I'll wake up early and get it over with.

The speaker on the elevator, unused for years, crackled slightly. White noise coming from nothing, broadcast through a rusted pit of a pinhole in the ceiling. High fucking quality living situation.

I'll ask Bennett where he lives tonight, if he's up. If he's not, after I pay rent.

The room lurched to a stop with all the elegance of the unoiled motor at the top. The brassy doors jerked open with the same kind of rattly inelegance, to the same hallway Kyle had come home to for so long.

The old red carpet at the end of the hallway was no longer faded, as it had been soaked through with buckets of fresh, red blood. Gillespie was dead at the bottom of the window frame, their body torn open and left to fester in the dark. Ribbons of gore ran up the walls, framing a short and thin man all in formerly blue clothes. He was barefoot and open-vested, his breasts hanging from an open button-up shirt. Kyle's neighbor, Ripley.

He raised his eyes to Kyle, away from the hatchet he was wiping clean.

"Hey, Kyle," he muttered in a quiet, high-pitched mumble.

Didn't wanna wake the neighbors, I guess.

"Hey, Ripley," she responded, far more tired than afraid.

"Sorry about the mess."

He waved vaguely at the hacked-up corpse of their landlord on the floor with his axe. The metal was already re-polished to a mirror sheen, as if it were a showpiece, not a murder weapon.

"You're okay," she muttered, stopping in front of her door. She nonchalantly pulled out her phone. You know, for the RFID for her room's lock.

"They came up saying I was late on rent that I paid last week," Ripley grumbled.

"Yeah, they do that."

The tone between them was congenial. Neighbors who'd never had strife, save maybe a noise complaint one way or the other at the drunkest times. Kyle placed her phone and her bag of food on the floor in front of her apartment door and walked over to stand next to Ripley's side. The latter placed his axe on the ground behind him, and it clattered quietly to rest in the corner. Kyle spoke, cool as ice.

"I have a vagina now, apparently."

Ripley crossed his arms and tilted his head, his scruff of short, thick hair flopping from one side to the other.

"Oh really, now? What do you mean apparently?"

"I got dicknapped in an alleyway."

"Really? They stole your dick?"

"Dick and balls, sir."

Ripley shook his head disapprovingly.

"The things people will do these days. I bet they were real nice to you, too."

Kyle snorted and slid her hands into her jacket's front pockets.

"Yeah, you know. They/them pronouns, gets under your skin all nice like."

"Awful. I'm so sorry. You want a hug?"

Kyle lifted her right hand in a polite 'no.'

"I've gotten enough blood on me for a day. And *out* of me, even."

Ripley laughed and brushed uselessly at his shirt, a gesture more for comedy's sake than anything. Kyle glimpsed, for a second, why his boobs were hanging out - a sports bra, ripped down the middle.

Landlord probably grabbed it and ripped it when they were getting murdered. Neat.

Wolf-girl pointed down at the corpse, then flipped her hand palm-up.

"Need help with the body?"

"I thought you said you'd had enough blood on ya?"

Kyle rolled her eyes.

"I'm just thinking I don't wanna smell rot in my room for however long until someone finally snitches."

Ripley leaned to one side and picked up his axe again, swung it forward, and let the flat back of the head come to rest against his narrow shoulder.

"I'm gonna spend an hour or two hacking them up, then I'll go dissolve what's left in the pool in the backyard. I'll send the mush to the recomb, and we'll get Gillespie back in a month or so. Probably a lot less likely to be so pushy about money at one in the morning, too."

Kyle blinked, her eyes suddenly very, very sore. The time was a lot more pressing than the details of her landlord's imminent processing.

"What time is it? Fucking two or something?"

"Something like that. Better go eat dinner and sleep, Kyle. Sounds like you've had a hell of a day."

With a deft flick of his wrist, Ripley let his axe swing from his shoulder to let the blunt back gently tap against Kyle's groin.

"Welcome to the club, Orlanski."

Kyle smiled wide. A broad, incredulous grin.

"Fuck you, Ripley," her words barely audible through a choked-back laugh.

"I'll get a strap," he responded with a wink.

Kyle open-mouth snap-laughed, then backed up quickly back to her room's doorway. Phone in one hand, bag in the other, she unlocked the door, and stepped inside, away from the repeating, meaty *thwack* of Ripley's axe through the former Gillespie's meat.

"Bennett, I'm home," she muttered, quiet enough to be heard, but not so loud as to wake him, should he be asleep.

"Oh, welcome home," his tiny voice came. He was still on the couch, half-tucked under the corner of the blanket she'd left him with. Kyle slid her phone back into her pocket, checked the lock behind her, and then started shifting out of her jacket. It weighed like the world the moment she shifted it off one of her shoulders.

God, I'm tired.

Bennett perked his voice up a little louder, assured that nobody else could hear them.

"Bored without me for the past how-long?"

Kyle snorted, passing the brown sack to her other hand so she could shift the rest of that lead fucking denim coat of zero colors to the floor. It fell with a meaty enough thump that her ears twitched forward.

"More than you know, little buddy."

She bent down at the waist and pulled the knots on her bootlaces. They were already worn enough from a day of riding and stomping around that she didn't need to loosen the laces before pulling her feet from their brutally tight confines. Instantly, her legs started to throb with exhausted pain. She grimaced and turned her head toward her little squatter.

Guess I'd better ask, before I can't think.

"So," Kyle mumbled, "now that you're sober. Do you remember where you live?"

Bennett lowered his snout, an obvious look of guilt marring his pretty-boy face. His voice was quiet, even for his size.

He's about to say he's homeless.

"I'm homeless. I just kind of meander from place to place. Got kicked out of my old place when I broke up with my boyfriend at the time."

Kyle shrugged her shoulders.

Yeah, figures.

"Alright. You can crash here for a while, then."

He smiled timidly.

"Thanks, Kyle."

"No problem. Kinda fitting after all of today."

Bennett shifted and pulled his legs out from under the blanket, turned to face her and sat up. He tried being a little playful;

"Cathartic, maybe?"

"Catharsis is fake."

Some undefeated cruel spark of her almost told him about catharsis being some ancient Greek bullshit they teach you in Classical Studies and then neglect to contextualize and deprogram with literally any Humanities course. Nobody with an education that would actually make them money knew shit otherwise.

"That's fair," the tiger said, lacing his fingers together over his stomach.

"Cool."

She turned and sat on the other end of the couch, trying not to jostle him too much with the tidal force of her seven-foot-tall body and flat ass. The crinkle of the full brown bag coming to rest on the table was the most comforting thing in the world. Bennett sat up, leaning on his palms behind him.

"Smells good. Did you steal from the same place as this morning - or whenever, I guess?"

It smelled like a hollow victory. The promise of a greasy meal that wouldn't upset her delicate biochemistry, both new and old. The most stock-fucking-standard thing in the world was the burger and fries quietly, assuredly, seeping grease through their packaging, through the bottom of the bag, to leave a stain on the cheap, unlacquered table beneath. Appealing, abhorrent.

Fuck if that ain't a metaphor for something.

"No," she lied, "but I did steal it."

"Works for me."

Kyle hunched forward and opened the bag and let the comforting artificial smell of normalcy fill the room. The burger was exactly the same as the one that morning. The fries were, too. It was so fucking fake. It was perfect.

"Buncha shit happened today," she started, ripping open the bag to get at the juicy garbage inside. Wolf-girl lived up to her misnomer of a nickname and took no care in the way she mutilated this meal. One pinch of the burger, one bite of the fry, both arrayed haphazardly on a folded-up napkin for Bennett's late-night pleasure.

"Tell me about it," he responded, picking up his small-sized sandwich.

"Saw someone get hit by a train."

"That's neat."

"Yeah, it was a sex thing."

"Usually is, Kyle."

"Yeah."

She paused to take a big bite of her burger. Visions of gore flashed in her mind's eye as she ripped into it and gulped it down. Kyle felt hot - not like, sexy, necessarily - *Maybe a little bit.* - but physically. Like despite getting cleaned off at the doctor's, that there was an unusual amount of sweat and grease in her fur. Baking under her skin.

Kyle paused to chew and swallow before speaking.

"Sorry, spacing out a little. You know, slime time."

She saw Bennett put down his crushed burger and extend both hands toward her.

"No, Kyle, I *don't* know slime time. Can you fucking tell me what that meant? You said it earlier! Before the first time we ate, even!"

Kyle inhaled, worked a bit of gristle out of her molar with her tongue, and began.

"You know when you don't sleep for a while? Or sleep very little? You get tired enough that your emotions just kinda fuck off? That the events happening around you just kinda glaze over you? And when the sun comes up, it's just a little too hot? And you sweat just a little too much? And you can't ever drink enough, or smoke enough, or eat enough? And you're just so damn tired and greasy?

I call it slime time. You feel like you're just coated in it, you know?"

Bennett nodded slowly. A real 'I totally don't get this' kinda nod.

Yeah, figures.

"Anyway, I just wanna eat and sleep."

She took another thick bite of her burger. Bennett couldn't help but quip.

"Right now, or in general?"

"Both," she mumbled through a mouthful of ground beef and tangy condiments. The tiger visibly shivered.

Oh, he wishes that were him so fucking bad.

"Went down to the Circus and Hell. Ate a chick."

The most wonderful woman I will ever meet.

"Oh, jealous."

"Aren't you just. Anyway, I got paid to drag a corpse to a clinic."

"Easy money, right?"

Worst experience of my life.

"Oh, totally. Too bad I got assaulted in the alleyway."

"Oh shit?"

"Hacked my cock off. Had to go to a clinic and get a vag."

Bennett had to pause for a moment to process.

Me too, bud.

"Well," he started carefully, "I guess the fact that you're sitting here and chatting about it while you eat instead of sobbing means you're a lot harder of a person than I gave you credit for. Do you… I don't know, want to talk about it?"

I will talk to you so much, you little fuck. I will make you regret that offer every day for the rest of your life. I will sob onto your tiny shoulder and drown you in my tears. I will scare you away with every new exposed wrinkle of my trauma.

"Nah. I'm cool," Kyle lied, before immediately choking down the last bite of her burger.

"Brave of you. But... I know we haven't known each other long, but... well."

Bennett had finished his fraction of a burger too, and so patted his legs invitingly with both hands.

"I'm here."

Kyle grinned maliciously.

"For how long?"

She loved to imagine what she looked like from Bennett's eyes. This towering mountain of awkwardly hunched canine terror, fur as black as a starless night, eyes vicious and burning.

I probably just look sad and tired.

Kyle winced a little.

"As long as you'll let me be," he returned softly.

Oh, I'm just a prick.

With the last of the napkins, Kyle brushed as much grease and food detritus off her gnarled hands as she could. There were always crumbs in the fur unless she washed them, but it'd do for now. A little of the nerve she'd used earlier with Violet worked its way up from her heart to her mouth.

"Then, uh, can I hold you?"

Bennett blinked. Kyle blinked.

"I just think it'd be nice. I've had a rough day. I think you might like it, too."

"You're not wrong, Kyle," he responded.

Wolf-girl cupped her palms together and slid her fingertips very slightly under the pillow she'd let him sleep on all day. He stood with remarkable alacrity for having seemingly slept for the entire time she'd been awake, drugged or not. He practically pounced from the cotton into the matted-down scruff between her paw pads, and dramatically rolled to his knees at the end of his stunt.

"Impressive, just like all the other fleas," Kyle snickered.

"Oh shut up."

She upgraded to a laugh, and Bennett hissed one out too. Kyle let her eyes relax a little, now that she could safely hold onto her charge. She slid forward and slumped to the floor, her back against the front of her bed-couch.

"You know, uh… it's nice. It's nice to hold someone like this, I guess."

Her eyes fluttered a little. Warm food and a former lover laying down in your hands is better than Suvorexant.

"It's nice to *be* held, too. That's why I chose to *be* small."

"Intimate power imbalance, yeah?"

Bennett smiled softly and crossed his hands over his belly. He rested his head against the pad of her palm just below her fingers, like it were a leathery pillow. Kyle gingerly placed her other palm on top of him, like a heavy, fluffy blanket.

"Kyle, I really do enjoy the time we have together. Especially the time… at the party."

Blasting music, a frightened man on the table. My drool dripped around him. Slavering for his flesh. I could see there were tears in the corners of his eyes by the glimmer from the party lights. Phenomenal actor. I managed not to throw up until I got home. Cleaned him up with a dust broom and two plastic baggies.

"Yeah, that was a lot of fun," she muttered. Her voice was leaving her in her exhaustion.

"If you… you know, ever want to again…"

"Probably, little guy. Definitely not now."

"*Definitely* not now."

They sat in silence for a few minutes. A few hours. Something like that. You know how slime time is. Something gnawed at the bottom of her lungs, though. A familiar knot of guilt that threatened to grip at everything unless she spoke it aloud.

"Hey. Bennett, am… uh,"

He opened his eyes and frowned. She continued with a croak;

"Am I an awful person?

A lingering, pregnant moment.

"Yeah. So am I. You live with it."

Kyle sighed every iota of air out through her nose. She wanted to cry so badly. It had been a fucking awful day, two days, whatever the *fuck*. She felt so gross, so empty, physically, emotionally, mentally.

Instead, she still cradled her new and only friend in her palms and closed her eyes. The feverish ache of too many thoughts for one waking stretch blurred the lines between consciousness and dreams, dreams no more comforting than the firm, fake wood of couch she leaned against.

Fitful peace, before whatever came the next day. Horrible uncertainty, insecurity, fear of the malignant gray future swallowing her and Bennett up. Her throat choked up.

At least she knew, in the gaps between nightmares, she wouldn't ever go hungry.

Small, bitter laughs through the tears.

Special thanks to Finley Sinclaire for the front cover art.
Special thanks to Ramona W. for the back cover art.